To Save a Lost Soul

Tempie W. Wade

To Save a Lost Soul

By Tempie W. Wade

First Edition Print - ISBN: 978-1-7363975-8-9

Digital Edition - ISBN: 978-1-7363975-9-6

For more information, please visit,

www.TempieWade.com

To Save a Lost Soul

Tempie W. Wade

A Timely Revolution Prequel

1

CHAPTER ONE

Scotland

October 1585

Laird Colin MacLeod sat at the head of the table in the grand hall next to his new bride, Sabina. A lively jig played in the background, the wine flowed freely, and every guest seemed to be genuinely enjoying the celebration — apart, that is, from the two guests of honor. The groom glanced over at his new wife. A contemptuous groan escaped him as he reached for his cup. Leaning over, she whispered something behind her hand to her younger sister, Nahla. Noticing his gaze upon her, she glared back and turned away from him coldly. "The feeling is mutual, my dear," he muttered to himself and polished off another glass of whiskey—his fifth since the ceremony. Closing his eyes, he wondered how many more it would take to muddle his mind and get him through the rest of the 'celebration'. He had made certain there would be no wine for him—only the strongest libations would do for this reluctant husband on this miserable occasion.

Stewart MacLeod came up behind his son's chair and clasped both hands on his shoulders. "Cheer up, son, it's no' so bad," he whispered in his ear. "She is a bonnie lass, and ye could have done a great deal worse."

Colin craned his neck to look back at his father, screwing up his face. "Easy words for you to say, you weren't the one who was forced to marry her."

Stewart gripped him tightly. "I know ye are not happy about this union but joining our family with the MacDonnell's will ensure our lands and our people are safe for generations to come. Yer sacrifice for this marriage is but a wee price to pay for that."

"Besides," said his brother with a forced smile, raising a toast in the direction of his new sister-in-law, "it's not like she isn't quite lovely."

Colin sighed and frowned down at his empty glass. Lifting his head, he searched for one of the servants to refill it. "She is lovely, yes, and blessed with the temperament of a shrew sent straight up from the bowels of Hell to torment me. May God help me!" He managed to catch the attention of a boy who was refilling the goblets of the guests and shook his empty glass in his direction. The boy, having been well schooled on his duties, quickly set down the pitcher of wine he was carrying, picked up a bottle of whiskey, and hurried to fill the Laird's demand. "Perhaps I will get lucky and one of the men will take enough pity on me to run me through with a sword before I have to lay with her."

Stewart held up his hand and shooed the approaching servant boy away. "Ye have had more than enough to drink, son. This bargain is not complete until the union is consummated, and I need ye to be 'up' for the job, so to speak. Take no more drink, perform yer husbandly duties, and put a MacLeod heir in that lass's belly as quickly as ye can. The peace between our families will remain uneasy at best until a bairn comes from your marriage and unites us all. After that, ye can take as many whores on the side as ye wish, and I won't even give ye any grief over it."

Stewart returned to his seat next to Aenghus MacDonnell, the father of the bride, and cut his eyes toward Sabina. Gesturing his son with a nod of the head, he indicated he should get to work without further delay.

Filled with a sense of dread and palpable loathing, he took notice of Brody's full glass of whiskey. Colin angrily snatched it from his brother's hand and drank it down in one gulp.

"Hey!" exclaimed Brody, throwing up his hands in frustration.

Colin slammed the glass down and steadied himself. Sliding back his chair, he stood and slapped his hands flat on the table. The room instantly quieted. He wiped his mouth with the back of his hand and tried to force something resembling a pleasant expression on his face. "My dear guests," he announced while cutting his eyes at his father, "I would like to thank you all for sharing in the uniting of our two families here today, but if you will excuse us, the time has come for my wife and I to take our leave for the evening to make this marriage truly official."

The room erupted in applause and boisterous laughter filled the room.

Colin reached for his bride's arm, helped her from her chair, and waved his hand toward the stairs leading up to the special bed chamber that had been prepared for the evening. "Might as well get it over with," he mumbled under his breath.

Glowering, she angrily whipped her gown around, stepped in front of him, and stalked across the floor, going out of her way to make it clear that she was undesirous of his touch.

Colin shook his head and slowly followed, mentally preparing himself for the inevitable 'deed', stopping at every opportunity along the way to accept offers of 'congratulations' and proffered cups of alcohol. It was going to be a long night, and he needed all the liquid encouragement he could get.

Sabina was already stretched out rigidly on the bed wearing only her shift by the time he made his way into the room. He slowly pushed the door closed behind him, having to steady himself on the doorway before moving to the foot of the bed. The bridegroom was far from enthused by the circumstances he found himself in, or the woman who was now legally his wife, but he was determined to at least not make things any worse than they already were. In fact, he had decided he would go out of his way to make the best out of the situation.

Colin blew out a deep breath as he loosened his cravat and untied the collar of his shirt. "Are you familiar with what happens now? I know you have not had a mother to advise you since you were a child but has someone at least told you what to expect the first time you lay with a man?" he asked with as much compassion as he could muster.

"Just be done with it and leave me be," she spat. "I don't want ye touching me any longer than ye must!"

He pulled his shirt over his head and tossed it to the floor. "I will be gentle with you and do my best to make sure the pain is minimal. I do not wish your first time to be an unpleasant experience for you and, in the days ahead, I hope you might even come to find it enjoyable."

She laughed contemptuously while staring up at the ceiling and spat, "Ye think this is my first time? I would never let a man I do not love, much less one whose touch repulses me, have the satisfaction of taking my maidenhead. I will have THAT much control over my life if nothing more!" She yanked up her shift, rolled over on her stomach, and buried her face in the bedcovers. "Make it quick and leave me be so I don't have to look upon ye any longer this night."

Colin froze. His blood ran cold as the venom-filled words that spewed from her mouth caught him off guard and cut him straight through to the bone. He bent forward, grasped the hem of her gown, and snatched it down to cover her bare bottom.

"You can go," he said dismissively and moved to a nearby table that held a decanter of whiskey.

Her eyes flew open, and she pushed up on her arms. "What?" she demanded.

Colin pulled the stopper out and poured himself a glass. "I will not force myself upon a woman who does not desire me, even if she is my wife. I will give you as much time as you need to develop some civility toward me and to warm up to the idea of our marriage for the sake of our future children, but until that day comes, I will take my comfort elsewhere. Make no mistake, THAT day must come soon, or our families will be at war, and it will be a bloody battle that will take many lives on both sides. So, for now, feel free to get in that bed and go to sleep while you rest assured that I will not accost you or take you against your will."

"Oh aye, ye will take me!" she shouted. "My father has told me that if I do not lay with ye by morning that he will slit my throat, make ye a widower, and replace me with my sister as yer new wife. She is only thirteen, and I will never let that happen." She rolled off the bed and went to stand in front of him. "Ye WILL have me this night, one way or another, HUSBAND!"

He stepped away from her, took a seat in an oversized chair near the fireplace, and sipped his whiskey. "Nay, I will not and besides, no one will ever know except you and I that the 'deed' was not done, dear WIFE!"

A noise that came from behind one of the walls caught their attention. Colin suddenly remembered the reason they were put in the 'special' chamber for the night. A small room had been built on the other side, its entrance concealed by a wall panel in the hall, so that clergy and families could assure that marriages had been consummated by watching from a hidden peephole. It was a barbaric ritual, but their union would not be valid if he were not witnessed 'taking' her. And now according to his bride, if he didn't, she would be dead by morning.

"Bloody fecking hell!" he groaned and dropped his head into his hand.

Sabina's eyes widened anxiously when she heard her father's voice coming from the other side. She dropped to her knees in front of him. Sliding her hands beneath his tartan, she touched his manhood with her fingers and skillfully began to massage him.

Colin's body instinctively responded. He became firm and aroused to the point the glass slipped from his hand, landing on the floor. Pushing his tartan up around his waist, she exposed him completely and lowered her lips to touch the tip of his phallus with her tongue. Firmly wrapping her hand around his shaft, she began moving her hand up and down as she licked, teased, and tasted him until he was on the verge of losing all control.

It became painfully obvious to Colin his virgin bride was greatly experienced and knew exactly what she was doing. He grasped her by the wrists and pulled her up to prevent her from proceeding any further.

"Stop," he said softly, but the alcohol had begun to dull his mind, and his resolve was rapidly weakening. Sensing his vulnerability from the drink, she stood, pulled her shift up around her waist, and positioned her knees on either side of him, before slowly lowering herself onto his erection. She winced and cried out in pain, hoping to give the appearance of her virginal seal having just been breached for the first time for the audience on the other side of the wall.

She gripped the back of the chair with her hands and leaned forward. "Feck me, PLEASE!" she begged pitifully in his ear, glancing toward the wall, now on the verge of tears. "He will kill me by the morning if ye do not. My father is not a good man, and he will not think twice about doing it. I am your wife now, and ye vowed before God to protect me at all costs."

Colin could not in good conscience see her murdered simply because he refused her, after all, she was indeed his wife and his responsibility now. He wrapped his arms around her waist and rested his forehead on her shoulder. Given how well she had worked him up moments before, it was only a matter of a few thrusts before his seed exploded inside of her. He stood with his arms still around her and whispered, "Wrap your legs around me." She did as she was told, and he moved to deposit her on the bed with his back to the group that watched. Lightly touching his lips to hers, he used one hand to remove the small blade that he wore at the front of his belt. Inconspicuously, he slit his other palm and ran that hand down to smear her womanly parts, her inner thighs, and his manhood with his blood. After sheathing the knife, he stepped back and turned so that their unwanted audience could get a better look. He wrung out a wet rag from a water basin on the nightstand that was used for washing, lifted his tartan, and cleaned the blood from his member in plain view. Now, there would be no doubt in anyone's mind his bride had been a virgin on her wedding night and they had both performed their duties.

They heard laughter, offers of compliments, and good wishes from behind the partition, as well as the sound of the spectators leaving.

Once they were sure they were gone, Sabina got up and cleaned herself before pulling her gown down. She turned to Colin. "I suppose I should thank ye for that," she said haughtily, "but know that is the first and last time ye will ever touch me."

Any hopes Colin had for a civil union instantly dissipated from his mind. "Do you mean to tell me you do not intend to ever share my bed, not even occasionally?" he asked, spitefully, "You do understand that you are expected to give me an heir!"

She turned and glared at him. "Then ye had better pray ye put one in my belly this very night. I love another, and I will never lay with ye again."

He grabbed her by the arm. "That was not part of our marital arrangement. The MacLeod family needs our name to be carried on and you, as my wife, are expected to do your part. The only reason I agreed to this was so that you could give me bairns to keep the peace between our families."

She jerked her arm free. "I never agreed to that! As a matter of fact, I was not consulted about any of this. I was simply whored out by my father because my mother had the misfortune of giving him only girls, and he needed me to get something that he wanted."

Fury rose within him. "Maybe I will just go tell your father of your little escapades with another man, or men, given your seemingly vast experience. How do you think he will feel about your plans to not hold up the MacDonnell's end of the bargain?"

Sabina moved her face closer to his. "Go ahead, but he won't believe ye." She pulled the dagger from his belt, still covered in his blood, and held it up to his face. "After all, I was a virgin on my wedding night, and I have a roomful of witnesses to prove it. In fact, I was the one who had to initiate ye to act for our union, or did ye forget about that part? They all looked on as I took ye in hand because ye showed no interest in me whatsoever. In his eyes, I am the dutiful daughter doing all I can, even though I am saddled to a man who needs help to get his cock hard for a woman. Ye are just another MacLeod he doesn't give a shite about."

She tossed the knife onto the bed, sat down, and crossed her legs. "Your duty is done so ye can leave, or I will. It makes no difference to me."

Colin swallowed hard and walked out of the room, afraid of what he might do if he remained in her presence for even one more moment. He knew the situation was not ideal and neither of them wanted it, but as Laird of this castle, he needed to make a deal that benefited his family. He never would have agreed had he known how much contempt she truly held for him. Plenty of couples started with arranged marriages and things worked out well enough in the end, but it was as plain as the nose on his face this would not be the case in this instance. He cursed to himself when he thought about how she manipulated and tricked him into consummating the union—in front of everyone, no less. There was no way in hell he could get an annulment. He stomped out of the castle, into the darkness, and wandered until he found himself in his mother's garden, the one place he always went to when he needed to clear his head. The full moon shone down on her carved headstone and illuminated the words brilliantly.

Mary Asheton MacLeod

Beloved Wife and Mother

He began to wipe the stone with his hands. After he finished brushing the debris from the front of the marker, he sat down on the bench he had placed there not long after her death. He found himself spending more and more time there as of late, asking for her advice as he did when she was alive and hoping against hope for a response that never came.

"Mother, what have I gotten myself into and what am I going to do about it? I was only trying to do right by the people here and, in turn, I have condemned myself to a loveless marriage with a woman who cannot bear the sight of me. I have only been Laird for a short time, and I am already making a mess of things. This would have never happened if you were still here to guide me." The only response he received was the feeling of a gentle breeze caressing his face. Though no answer came to him, he still found it oddly comforting.

Colin sat in silence for nearly an hour trying to figure out a logical way out of his predicament. With no good solutions, he decided the best thing to do was to go back and try to somehow reason with her. If he could connect with her on some level, perhaps by commiserating over family duty and just talk to her, maybe they could find a way to tolerate each other and work something out, even if she were in love with another. He got up and slowly made his way back inside. Something in his mind urged him to seek out the advice of his brother instead.

He stopped outside of his room and knocked lightly on the door. "Brody? It's Colin. I need to talk to you. It's important." He heard the rustle of the sheets from inside and assumed his brother was getting out of bed to let him in. Colin placed his hand on the handle, turned the knob, and slowly cracked open the door.

Nothing prepared him for what he saw.

While the room was only dimly lit by candles, he could still make out the form of his brother with a woman. He was spread out on the bed, and her head bobbed up and down as she pleasured him. Not wanting to interrupt someone who was feeling the warm comfort of a woman on this night, Colin went to quietly back away and leave them to their business. It was then Brody's hands fell to the back of his lover's head, and he called out the unmistakable words — "Oh Sabina!"

Colin's blood ran cold. He exhaled sharply, hoping he was mistaken, but knowing he was not. He flung the door wide open, allowing the light from the candles in the hall to illuminate the room and the two lovers' faces. Rage overtook him, and his body began to violently tremble.

"Forgive the intrusion, but I think you are sucking the wrong brother's cock on your wedding night, my dear WIFE!" he spat.

The startled couple hastily ceased their actions and

scrambled off the bed.

"Colin —I can —explain—" stuttered Brody, searching for something to cover himself.

A furious Colin rushed him, slamming him into the wall, and pinning him with his forearm. Blood exploded from his knuckles when he punched the wall with his fist. "You are her lover? My baby brother? How dare you endanger our family and betray ME of all people. How long has this deceit been going on? How long have you been fecking that faithless whore?"

Brody slumped, refusing to fight back, and closed his eyes, his face full of remorse and humiliation.

"ANSWER ME!" Colin roared. "Confess to me NOW!"

"Since I went to the MacDonnell's home to make the arrangements," he said quietly.

"You allowed me, nay, stood up with me when I married this bitch and all this time, ye were having her under my nose and my roof?" Colin tightened his hold on Brody's throat until he began to struggle to catch his breath. "Did she bother to tell you those same lips licked my cock not an hour ago?"

Sabina screamed and attacked Colin, pounding him on the back and tearing at his shirt as she tried to get him away from her lover. "Leave him be! I love him. He is the only man I will ever want for as long as I live!"

Colin's attention shifted, and he turned, focusing his rage upon her. He released his grip on Brody long enough for him to crumple to the floor, clutching at his throat, desperately gasping for air.

"YOU!" Colin seized her around the waist and dragged her still naked form down the hall to their bedchamber. Once inside, he bolted the door and shoved her onto the bed. She pulled her knees tightly to her chest, wrapped her arms around them as her eyes welled, and waited for his wrath to rain down. He pointed at her. "Why did you agree to marry me if you only wanted to be with my brother?"

"I told ye," she cried, "my father gave me no choice. He despises me for being born a girl, and what I want is of no matter to him."

He leaned across the bed until he was in her face, nose-to-nose.

"After being played the fool this night, forgive me if I don't believe you. I have had quite enough of being toyed with in my own home by my new bride who will willingly spread her legs for my brother rather than me on OUR wedding night."

"It's true!" she sobbed, her eyes now red and swollen. "He couldn't wait to be rid of me."

He straightened up, standing at the edge of the bed. "Tell me why I shouldn't drag you downstairs to your father, tell him everything and let him deal with you as he sees fit? After all, you do have a perfectly good sister who can easily take your place and one who may decide she actually wants me in her bed. She might even miraculously be a virgin!"

"No! No! Please don't!" she crawled over to him and grasped at the tail of his shirt, sniveling. "Father will demand Brody and I both pay for this with our lives, and Nahla, she is too young to be your wife. Getting her with child at her age would kill her. Please! I beg you! I promised my mother on her deathbed I would always make sure my sister was safe." She began to weep and fell face down on the bed in a wail.

Colin took a good long look at the blubbering heap before him and a tiny part of him couldn't help but feel sorry for her. After he had forced himself to calm down, he reached for a blanket, bawled it up, and threw it at her. "Do you truly want to be with my brother so badly you could not stay away from him for one damn night?" He sat down on the bed beside her.

"More than anything," she whispered, pitifully, pulling the covers around her face tightly and peeking out.

"And what of our marriage and the children I was promised would be given to me? I am bound to a woman who can't stand the sight of me, who refuses to share my bed, and only wants to have relations with my brother. Which, by the way, I cannot allow to continue, especially under my own roof. And truthfully, after seeing your lips wrapped around Brody's cock on OUR wedding night, the thought of having you in my bed sickens me to my stomach. If by some chance you have already become with child from our union this night, or from another with him, there will always be a question as to who the father is. What are we going to do about this unfortunate set of circumstances we find ourselves in?"

He stood up when he saw the full decanter of whiskey on the side table, picked it up, and drank straight from the canister.

"Ye cannot hold me here forever!" she said and wiped her face with the back of her hand.

He pointed his finger at her and sighed, "That's where you are wrong, my dear wife." He pulled a chair up to the bedside and sat down. "You see, you are mine now in the eyes of the church and the law, and I am permitted to do whatever I wish with you, or to you, and you have no say in the matter. You need to understand, you are at the mercy of my whims and desires from this day forward."

"And what do ye intend to do with me?" she demanded.

He leaned back in the chair and eyed her. "That remains to be seen, but I am sure I can figure out an appropriate response for catching you in the act of sucking my brother's cock. Make no mistake, you will have to suffer the consequences for that act."

She wiped her face on the blanket and curled on her side in a ball away from him. Pulling the bed covering tight, she sobbed herself to sleep. He spent the rest of the night drinking and watching her until he finally passed out in a drunken stupor in the chair sometime before dawn.

The following morning, nursing a massive headache, Colin stumbled down the stairs for breakfast, leaving Sabina in bed asleep. His little sister, Skye, and her husband, Finn, were the only ones in the dining hall when he made his way in.

"You look like hell!" Skye eyed him warily. "Did your wedding night not live up to your expectations?" she asked, cautiously.

"Not all of us have the luxury of running off to marry someone we love and getting to live happily ever after in a cottage by the sea!" he snapped before shouting for someone to bring him whiskey.

"It's a little early for that, don't you think?" Skye suggested.

"It's never too early for whiskey, especially when you have had a night such as I have."

"I take it the experience did not live up to yer expectations?" inquired Finn with a sly smirk before spearing a piece of food with his fork. "Was the virgin bride a little less than 'warm and welcoming'? Ah, well, wedding nights can sometimes be a little overwhelming. I am sure ye two will successfully manage to overcome your obstacles in the days to come, after all, ye have the rest of your lives to make up for it."

Colin cut his eyes at Finn before craning his head toward the door. "Where the hell is my drink!" he bellowed.

An older woman shuffled out of the next room with a glass

in one hand and a bottle in the other. "Hold yer horses! I am coming as fast as I can! Ye may be Laird of this castle, but that doesn't magically make ME any younger or faster, ye wee little shite. Remember who ye are squawking at before I lop off yer ear!"

"Thank you, Molly," he softened a bit when he saw she was the one answering his call. She finally reached the table and slammed the glass and bottle down directly in front of him before smacking him on the back of the head. Molly had been there forever and a day and, at the ripe old age of eighty-two, she still ruled the roost, along with their hearts.

She leaned with one hand on the table and the other on her hip. "What's the matter? Having a wife who hasn't already had half of Scotland between her legs already not to yer liking? Did she interfere with last night's whoring too much?" she mocked before turning and going back toward the kitchen, muttering, "I'm guessing the great Laird wouldn't be in such a foul mood if that lass had sucked yer—" she trailed off as she went around the corner.

His jaw tightened. "Oh, she's been 'had' plenty, trust me," he mumbled.

Finn chuckled behind his hand.

Skye's eyes widened. "It sounds like there is a great deal more to this story. I think you had better tell us what is going on, brother."

Before he could offer a response, his father came into the room, smiling and in a jovial mood. "Oh good, ye are here! I trust ye had a pleasant night," said Stewart.

A look of disgust crossed Colin's face, and he turned his head to look in the other direction.

"Where is Brody?" asked his father. "I have news he needs to hear."

Colin closed his eyes and gritted his teeth. "I am not my brother's keeper! If you want to have a word with him, find him yourself."

Skye and Finn exchanged curious looks.

"Oh well, he will hear it soon enough," he said, pulling out a chair to sit down. "After the festivities last night, MacDonnell and I had a nice long discussion, and we have decided that Brody will take Nahla as his wife."

"Nahla?" exclaimed Skye. "Father! She is a mere child!"

"She is old enough to bleed and give him a son, and that is all that matters," he replied.

Colin glared at his father. "Enlighten me! What was the payment for her? Aenghus MacDonnell gives nothing away for free, least of all one of his daughters. What will be the cost on our part for this joyous union?"

Stewart waved his hand dismissively. "Just a fortification and some of the surrounding land in the western part of our holdings. Nothing that will be missed."

"Land closest to their lands that gives them an advantage in a fight, no doubt!" Colin slammed his fist on the table. "I am Laird of this land, and I was not consulted. This is not a deal I am willing to make. I forbid it!"

Stewart looked down at the table and rubbed a nonexistent spot with his finger. "I am only making these matches to strengthen yer rule as Laird, and ye should be more grateful for what I have done! Since there will be no fighting between our families now that we are joined, ye have nothing to be concerned about."

Colin's face reddened as he seethed. "Taking an arranged wife as Laird is a given, and a responsibility I willingly accepted, but there is no good reason for Brody to take one, especially one who is thirteen and still plays with dolls, for Christ's sake. It's bad enough I have to endure this God-awful misery; I will not force it upon anyone else under my protection!"

His father leaned back in his chair. "Ye are correct, son. The final decision is yers but creating strife with yer new in-laws so early in the marriage is not something I would recommend." Stewart rose from his chair and as he walked past his son, he stopped. "Just make sure yer wife is well with child before the seasons change. Seal this pact once and for all, for all our sakes." On that note, he left the room.

Anger gripped Colin; his glass shattered in his hand.

Skye leapt from her seat and rushed to his side, taking his

bloody hand in hers to examine it. It was then she noticed the dried blood on his knuckles. "Bring me some rags and some clean water!" she called out to Molly, then looked to Colin. "What in God's name happened last night? What are you not saying?"

He looked up at her with a detestable look on his face. "My wife has decided she prefers to warm another's bed, and it appears to be our brother's."

Skye slowly sank down in a chair. "Are you certain?"

"I caught them in the act in his chamber on our wedding night."

Finn stopped Molly at the doorway and took the towels and a bowl of water before sending her back to where she came from. He brought them over, and Skye used them to clean his hand.

"Well, I could have thought of a thousand other, more appropriate, wedding gifts!" smarted Finn, a curious grin on his face. "When ye say, 'in the act', what exactly did you see? I think we need a few more details before we jump to any conclusions." A mischievous gleam appeared in his eye.

Skye shot him a scathing look, but Finn was only encouraged by her attention. He blew his lover a sweet kiss dissolving her annoyance instantly. She couldn't help but smile.

"What are you going to do?" she asked, turning her attention back to Colin.

Colin simply shook his head. "There is nothing I CAN do.

She and I are legally wed with no hope of annulment, and if word of this gets out, there will never be peace between our clans, because one side will always blame the other. She has also made it abundantly clear if she did not conceive last night, there will never be another chance. If she has somehow managed to become with child, I will have to raise it as my own even though I will always question who the father truly is."

Finn scratched the back of his head. "Wait, ye and she did the deed, and then she went straight to your brother's bed, and they—"

Colin made a wry face.

Finn winced. "Allow me to offer my sincerest condolences on your nuptials. I have known a few emboldened women in my time, but she may be an even rarer breed. That woman very well may have bigger balls than—well, ME!"

"FINN!" scolded Skye. "You are not helping!"

When she finished nursing his hand, Skye leaned forward and took her brother by the shoulders. "Colin, this isn't right. Why should you endure this? As our older brother, you have always put me and Brody first, no matter what the personal cost to you, but THIS is too much to ask of anyone. After all you have done for this family, you deserve to find some happiness, and at the very least, you should have a faithful wife whose heart belongs to you and no one else. There has to be something that can be done."

Colin pressed his forehead to her shoulder and let out a deep, burden-filled sigh. "Believe me, I wish there was a way, but I can think of no other option."

The look of despair on Skye's face for her brother's predicament was more than Finn could stand, having never been able to bear to see her in distress…and he felt the need to step in.

"Well, maybe there is something ye can do." He sat down in the chair and decided to offer a little friendly advice to his brother-in-law.

An hour later, Colin sat at his desk staring into nothingness as he rested his bandaged hand on the arm of his chair.

Brody silently made his way inside the room to stand before the Laird with his hands clasped before him and his head bent in shame.

Colin slowly shifted his gaze to his little brother, the one he had watched over, loved, and protected since he entered this world —the same one that had betrayed him in the worst possible way.

"I don't know what to say to you, brother," whispered Brody as his eyes welled. "I have committed an unforgivable act, and I willingly offer you my life in atonement to do with as you deem fit. I only hope that one day before you depart this world for the next, you find it in your heart to forgive me, even though I know

I do not deserve it."

Colin sat stone-faced for a long while before he finally reached over and poured two glasses of whiskey. "SIT!" he ordered and pushed one of the glasses in front of him. "DRINK!"

Brody unhurriedly sat down on the chair, took it in hand, and stared down into the amber liquid. "Poison is it? Well, I must thank you for a quick death, brother. It is certainly far more than I deserve." He drank it down, rested the glass on the desk, and closed his eyes to wait for the inevitable, resigned to his fate.

"It's not poisoned, you idiot!" Colin jeered and drank down half of his own.

Brody let out a momentary sigh of relief before squaring his shoulders. "Then tell me how I shall meet my demise."

"I don't want your life!" he snapped. "Least of all over a faithless whore!"

"Please do not speak ill of her," Brody whispered with his eyes cast downward. "I take full responsibility for all of this. It is my fault, not hers."

Colin rested his elbow on the arm of the chair with his cheek in hand staring at his brother, coming to a disturbing realization. "You stupid fool! You have fallen in love with her, haven't you?"

Brody nodded. "Since the day I first met her."

Colin leaned across the desk. "Why the feck didn't you tell me before I married her?"

"Father said if this marriage did not take place we would be at war with the MacDonnells before the end of the season, and you know as well as I do, it is not one we would win without great cost and far too many souls lost. What are my feelings over the lives of so many people? I made it clear to her I had no intention of being with her after you were wed, but she came to me last night speaking of her love for me and, God help me, my heart could not turn her away no matter how much my head said I should."

"Apparently, your cock couldn't turn her away, either," Colin mumbled under his breath. He smacked the desktop with his hand. "Father! Damn him and all these plans he is so hell-bent on carrying out. I am assuming he has not enlightened you about the little engagement he has arranged for you."

"What?" asked Brody, visibly taken aback. "What are you talking about?"

"He expects you to wed Nahla."

Brody's face paled. "Sabina's sister? The child?" He covered his face with his hands. "Oh, dear God, this cannot be! I feel like I am in a horrible nightmare from which I cannot wake."

"Well, that makes two of us." Colin fiddled with the whiskey bottle. "I forbade the marriage. It's bad enough I am bound to one I do not love and who despises me, but I will not condemn you, or anyone else, to the same damned fate."

"She does not despise you, only the situation. Her father is a brutal man, especially when it comes to his daughters."

"Which begs the question—what are we going to do about all of this?"

Brody wiped his nose with the back of his hand, appearing miserable. He let out a heavy sigh. "I know what I must do. I will leave here after I have convinced Sabina I never loved her— that I only used her for my pleasure. Perhaps, if I am cruel enough and no longer in the picture, the two of you can somehow find a way to at least become amicable toward each other."

"No, you will not!" Colin exhaled. "I will share a great many things with my little brother, but carnal knowledge of my wife is not one of them and besides, that will only make her resent me more. We will have to come up with another solution."

"Any other ideas?"

Colin sighed.

Colin avoided Sabina for the rest of the day, until they were forced to sit next to each other at supper in the grand hall. When it came time for them to retire for the night, he took her by the arm. "Come, wife! It is time for you to do your duty and please your husband," he announced loudly to the room. His remarks were met with a round of cheers and 'whoops'.

She forced a smile at him for the benefit of the others and stood.

He placed his hand on her back and escorted her to the bedchamber.

Once inside, she raced to the far side of the room and glared at him. "I already told ye I will never lay with ye again!"

He folded his arms, "And I told you; I can do whatever I wish with you because you have no say in the matter."

Her face grew fearful. "Ye mean to take me against my will, ye bastard? Is that what real men do? Is that what makes ye firm? The thought of forcing yerself upon an unwilling woman?"

"You didn't seem too unwilling when you were straddling me last night and begging me to feck you in front of your father!" He rolled his eyes. "And, by the way, wife, I would not take you again if my eternal soul depended on it." He turned when he heard a soft knock at the door and opened it to let Brody inside.

The younger man rushed to her and took her in his arms. "Hello, sweetheart!"

Sabina looked back at Colin, confused. "I don't understand. What is the meaning of this? Do ye mean to expose us to everyone downstairs?"

Colin pointed to the chair and motioned for her to sit.

Brody smiled and guided her over. "The Laird has come up with a plan for us to be together."

"What?" she asked, bewildered.

Colin leaned against the wall. "Your father and his men are returning home in the morning, and tomorrow night, you and my brother are leaving for one of our homes in the northern part of our lands. I will tell our father I sent Brody away because I caught word of some trouble, and I will tell everyone else you have not been feeling well since this evening. In a few weeks, I will send word to your father, and announce to everyone here, you passed unexpectedly from a fever, and we buried you immediately for fear of someone else becoming ill. You will have a nice cairn near the loch where I can adoringly leave flowers—or something of the such to pay my respects. After a period of mourning, I will be free to take another wife and you, and my brother, can live however you wish."

"What if someone comes to where we are going?" she questioned.

Brody took her by the hand. "No one ever goes to the northern part of our lands and, if they do, the house is equipped with secret rooms we can easily hide in for days. The staff there are loyal, and we will not be found out. If you do happen to be seen, we can just say your ghost haunts the place."

Sabina's hand flew to her face and tears sprang to her eyes. "Really? Ye and I can truly be together?"

Brody nodded. "Thanks to my brilliant brother, you will never have to fear your father again!"

Her face suddenly clouded over, and she looked to Colin. "What about Nahla? He will wish to marry her off to ye."

Colin shrugged. "I will simply say she is too young for my liking at this time, and I am not ready to wed again, to put him off for a while. By the time she is older, we will have figured something out, but I will ask him to send her here in the meantime, as a goodwill gesture, so she will be safe under our roof and away from him."

Sabina looked up at Colin. "Why are ye being so nice to me after the way I have scorned ye?" she asked, suspiciously.

"Because there is no point in all three of us being miserable, and no one deserves to be treated the way your father has treated you and your sister. Brody has filled me in on a few more of the details, and I can see why you felt the need to do as he ordered."

She jumped to her feet and threw her arms around his neck. "Thank ye, husband!"

Colin patted her on the back. "Now my 'not so dear' wife, if you will excuse me, I think I will leave the two of you alone and go find myself a nice willing woman in the village for the evening. You two are welcome to stay here tonight. Perhaps some pleasant sounds coming from this room will aid in our deception."

As he left the room, Brody stopped him and embraced him. "I love you, brother, and I am forever indebted to you. I cannot thank you enough."

Colin took his face in both hands. "I should be thanking YOU!" He kissed his face. "You are the one taking that horrible shrew off my hands!" He winked at Sabina, exited the room, and slipped out of the castle unnoticed.

Laird MacLeod whistled as he rode into town, grateful to be relieved of all marital duties for the night. As a matter of fact, with Finn's plan in play, he was looking forward to the days ahead with no wife to suffer. He preferred the company of the women he paid, mainly because it meant no worries and no responsibilities. If he had been given the choice, he never would have taken over as Laird, but as the eldest son, it all fell to him whether he wanted it or not.

Colin made his way around to the back of the brothel and tied his horse. Opening the door slowly, he looked around until his eyes fell upon the proprietor. When she saw him, she acknowledged him and waved him up the stairs to the room he frequented consistently. He undressed, climbed under the covers, and waited to see who would keep him company on this evening.

Calyn came into the room and crossed her arms. "Has the Laird tired of his bride already? It's only the second day!"

"You have no idea," he said and tossed back the covers, making room for her. "I don't want to think about her tonight."

"What's yer pleasure, then?" She crossed the room and dropped her robe.

"Surprise me! You know what I like!"

"Aye, I do!" Calyn joined him on the bed wearing only a smile.

Colin returned the following morning just before dawn in a

wonderful mood and was about to creep back into the bedchamber, when he heard it—a muffled cry and some shuffling from inside the room. He rushed in to see a ghastly pale and trembling Nahla sobbing while standing by the edge of the bed. Her gown was covered in blood, as were her hands and arms. She was also firmly grasping the handle of a knife.

"What the hell is going on here?" he demanded, wrenching the blade from her grasp. He felt himself go numb when his eyes drifted over and he saw his brother and his wife, both lying dead in the bed. "What did you do, you foolish child?" he demanded and tossed the knife aside. Slowly making his way over to the couple, he gently took his brother's now lifeless face in his hands. "Brody? Dear God, NO!"

"I heard them," she confessed, in a low, monotone voice. "I slipped into the secret room after I heard others talking about it, because I wanted to see what a man and woman did when they were in bed together, but I saw him through the peephole instead of ye. They were verra drunk and talking about how they were going to run away together. If they had done that, Father would have hunted them down, killed them both, and then married me off to ye. I only intended to scare him away, to plead with him to leave her alone, and to honor the marriage vows the two of ye exchanged. I waited until they were asleep and slipped in. I placed the blade to his throat, the way I have seen my father do to so many other men, and shook him to wake him, to tell him to go, but when his eyes opened, he was startled, and he fought back against me. The blade was sharp, and it slipped, slicing his throat open. I didn't mean to kill him, I swear it! When Sabina woke and saw what I had done, she was enraged and lunged at me before she saw the knife in my hand, falling onto the blade. It all happened so fast." Tears started to fall again as she looked down at the blood on her palms.

Colin pulled his brother's still warm body to his chest and rocked him as he wept. "BRODY! BRODY!" He cried out over and over before a wretched howl of grief erupted from deep in his chest.

Nahla looked at the devastation around her, realizing what she had done. She rushed from the room and was gone from sight before the mournful noise summoned the rest of the household. Stewart MacLeod and Aenghus MacDonnell were the first ones to reach the scene.

"What have ye done?" shouted Aenghus, moving to see his daughter's dead body in a pool of blood.

Colin was too overcome with shock and dismay to speak as his father rushed to his side. Brody and Sabina's bodies were both naked, and it was clear they had been lovers. Colin was covered in Brody's blood and the knife lay on the floor, just at his side.

"Oh my God!" choked Stewart, turning away from the gruesome sight, his heart broken by what he saw. "Son, how could ye have done this? She may have been a faithless whore, but how could ye kill yer own brother?"

"Ye call my daughter a faithless whore, but yer other son is the one in her marriage bed! If the Laird had been tending his wife this night, his brother would not have had a chance to sneak in here and have his way with my daughter!" spat Aenghus angrily. "What is certain is that none of the MacLeods can be trusted to hold to their word!" MacDonnell moved back into the hall and shouted for his men to pick up their arms. "My daughter has been murdered at the hands of her new husband. Any truce we had with the MacLeod family is over! Kill them all!"

Colin's senses returned to him when he heard those words uttered. "I didn't do this!" he mumbled as his gaze drifted down to the blood on his hands.

"Then who did?" demanded Aenghus, furiously. "Who else would have taken my daughter's life?"

Colin thought of that poor girl, who had obviously been traumatized by her father, and did not have the heart to give her up to him, not that he would believe him anyway. "I don't know, but it was not me! I would never do something like this to my little brother. I loved him too much!"

Soon, the ring of clashing swords and the screams of death reverberated throughout the entire castle. In the span of an hour, blood flowed freely from the floors to the grounds outside like a river, and the Laird Colin MacLeod lay on his back, dying from his massive wounds. As he struggled, a face he recognized unexpectedly appeared above him staring down at him intently. "Finn?" he whispered, blood spilling from the corners of his mouth.

Finn knelt and touched his shoulder. "Aye, it's me." He looked him over and frowned. "It will be over soon, and there shall be no more pain."

"Skye?" he asked. "Is she...?"

"Yer sweet sister is safely back at our cottage by the sea and is fine, but I am afraid no other members of your family were spared this day."

Colin coughed blood and it spewed into the air. "This is all my fault. I suppose I shall feel the flames of Hell soon enough for what wrongs I have committed in this life."

Finn looked around sadly. "This is not your fault at all, my dear boy. Ye deserve so much more, and this was merely an unfortunate series of events. But word of this will break your sister's heart just the same, and I have never been able to bear that woman's tears. I am afraid I love her too much to let her suffer from the shock of living with something like this." Finn took him by the hand and smiled as he recited a few words Colin did not understand. His hand slipped from Finn's, and he felt himself being pulled away from his body as a bright light appeared before him. He closed his eyes, said a silent farewell to his life, and let go—but when his eyes opened again, he found himself standing over his own lifeless body. Looking down, he came to the startling realization there would be no peaceful reward in the afterlife for him, nor would there be flames from Hell rising to singe his soul. Instead, the penance for his actions as Laird of this home would be to watch over it and its residents for all of eternity. With that, he let out an unearthly howl that shook the very ground and echoed throughout all of Scotland.

2
CHAPTER TWO

Scotland

October 2016

Willow Mason stood outside of the ramshackle establishment and wondered exactly what the holy hell she had gotten herself into. Her boyfriend, Ronnie, waited for the cab driver to remove their suitcases from the trunk of the car and paid him, before making his way over to her side.

"Are you sure this is the right place?" she asked. "It seems a little rundown for an inn that's hosting a weeklong event."

He looked down at the address on the screen of his phone. "Yep, this is it."

"I can't believe I let you talk me into this," she mumbled and moved toward the door, a 'welcome' sign hanging sideways by a single nail.

"What are you complaining about?" he asked, picking up his backpack and travel bag. "We get to stay a whole week in a castle in Scotland for free, plus we get paid a thousand dollars to boot. It's like a once-in-a-lifetime vacation. All you have to do is give a few readings while this paranormal crap is going on, and we can spend the rest of the time relaxing."

Willow owned a small spiritual store in Alexandria, Virginia, where she sold crystals, tarot cards, and candles, as well as offering private medium sessions in the back. Having been able to see spirits for as long as she could remember, she, thankfully, had a supportive mother who had guided her and showed her how to use her gift rather than having her committed to the nearest insane asylum. She had heard about these paranormal events, where people who fancied themselves amateur ghost hunters, would come out with their equipment and beg a spirit to turn on a light or speak a few words into a recorder as proof of life after death. Having always thought it a little ridiculous and over-the-top cheesy, she had been forced to reconsider when a gentleman came into the store, told her about an event in Scotland, and made her a cash offer to make an appearance.

At Ronnie's insistence, and with a stack of overdue bills, it became clear it was an offer she could not refuse. The shop had not been doing well as of late because of a downturn in the economy, and since Ronnie had lost his job at the car dealership, along with his apartment, she needed all the extra money she could get. Even more so now since he had somehow convinced her to let him move in with her.

"Don't forget your stuff!" he called over his shoulder as he opened the door and disappeared.

Willow looked back to see her suitcase left right where the driver had dropped it. She rolled her eyes and went to retrieve it before following him inside to the first room where sat a small check-in desk.

Ronnie rang the bell with the palm of his hand and an older gentleman shuffled around the corner, taking his own sweet time.

"Can I help ye?" he asked when he reached the counter.

"We have a room under the name of 'Mason'," replied Ronnie.

The old man shoved his glasses up on his nose and opened his reservation book. Stopping to lick his finger, he slowly flipped through a few pages searching for their information. "Mason, Mason, Mason," he mumbled as he looked up and down the pages. "Oh aye, here ye are!" he finally announced. "Willow Mason—ye are the psychic."

"Medium," corrected Willow, using her fingernail to pluck at the corner of a piece of faded wallpaper on the wall. "I don't see the future, just dead people."

"Well, ye are in the right place, my dear! We have plenty of those, if anyone asks this week, that is," he said with a wink. Clearing his throat, he held up an envelope. "The organizer of this paranormal bullshi—" he coughed, "I mean—paranormal event—asked me to give ye this schedule."

Willow accepted it from him and laughed. "I take it you are not a believer."

"Oh, I believe," he replied. "I believe in letting the dead rest in peace. I have found if I don't bother them, they don't bother me. Personally, I wouldn't let these people in here for all this nonsense, but they pay well and upfront, and we use all the money for upkeep around here." He looked around with a resigned face. "There's NEVER enough money for upkeep on old places like this, so we can't afford to turn anyone down."

He shook his head and placed an old-style key on the desk. "Ye are in the special 'Wedding Night Bedchamber Suite'."

"You hear that?" said Ronnie, seemingly impressed. "A special suite!"

"Aye, it is the most famous room in the castle," said the man, stacking some papers and tapping them on the desk to straighten them before putting them away.

"What's the story?" asked Willow, suddenly curious.

The old man took off his glasses and wiped his face with a handkerchief he produced from his pocket. "It is the room where the Laird Colin MacLeod caught his wife, of one day, in bed with his brother and brutally stabbed them both to death. That was the beginning of the end for the MacLeod family. The bride's father became so enraged by the sight of his murdered daughter, he ordered his men to kill every member of that family, the Laird being the last one to die in front of the fireplace in the main hall."

"That's horrible!" she said.

"It 'tis," the old man shook his head sorrowfully, as if truly upset by the history, "but with this newfound interest in chasing ghosts, it's also extremely good for business." He recovered quickly and pointed over his shoulder with his thumb. "Yer room is the last one at the end of the hall once ye reach the top of the stairs. Enjoy your stay!" he said and shuffled off.

Willow snatched the key and snarked at Ronnie. "Did you hear that? We are lucky enough to get the 'murder suite'! Yay us!"

"Why do you have to be like this?" he snapped. "It's a free trip for a few damn readings. It's not like it will kill you. Let's just go find our room and unpack."

Willow stood inside their home for the next few days and looked around. "Oh—my—God!" she slowly exclaimed. "I am fairly certain those are the original bedclothes!" She turned up her nose and warily pulled back the blood-red bedspread, stepping back when a single moth fluttered out.

"You would think they could have picked a better color," admitted Ronnie. He dropped his bags and went to a small table by the fireplace that held a tray with a bottle, two glasses, and a 'welcome' card. Reaching for it, and after reading the label, he waved it in the air. "Oh well, free scotch!"

"Thank God there is that at least," muttered Willow as she

roamed the room. "Where is the bathroom anyway?"

Ronnie located a small, laminated information book on the table. "It says here it is down the hall. We will be sharing with two other rooms."

"Are you kidding me?" she asked in disbelief. "We don't even have our own bathroom? What the hell kind of place is this?"

He pulled the cork from the bottle with his teeth and spat it onto the floor. "Don't you know anything about the world? It's a common thing overseas. We will survive! You know why? Because it's FREE!"

Willow shook her head and started out the door.

"Where the hell are you going?" he demanded.

"I need to get some air and clear my head! Enjoy your free scotch!"

Willow found herself outside wandering the grounds. Being inside made her feel as if she were being suffocated. Or maybe it had more to do with being around Ronnie. Dating him hadn't been so bad at first, even though he was never a 'Prince Charming,' but being with him all the time now was starting to wear thin on her nerves. She noticed a bench in the middle of a patch of overgrown rose bushes and made her way over to it to sit down.

She dropped her face into her hands and closed her eyes,

hoping to fend off a migraine that was trying to come on. Inhaling deeply, she turned her head to the side, and blinked, only to notice the corner of something incredibly old poking out from beneath the undergrowth. Getting up, she peeled back a few of the branches to get a better look at whatever it was.

Willow was more than a little surprised to see it was a gravestone. Curious, she pulled and tugged at the brambles, folding them over and carefully breaking off a few briars until the marker itself was cleared off. Kneeling respectfully, she brushed it off with her hands and used her finger to trace over the extremely worn lettering until she was able to make out what it said.

Mary Asheton MacLeod
Beloved Wife and Mother

Since she was already halfway there, she decided to clear away a few more sections around it, and when she was done, she noticed the rose bushes had been planted specifically in a pattern around the grave.

"Someone must have loved you very much, Mary Asheton MacLeod," she said aloud as she stood up and brushed off her knees. "That's better!" She smiled, pleased with her work and grateful for the distraction from her own problems. Willow felt the sudden urge to do one more thing. She plucked a lovely red rose bloom from the bush, inhaled the sweet fragrance, and placed it on the stone. "Rest well, Mary!"

Colin made his way through the main hall, and as he did, something caught his attention. It was a printed sign on an easel.

Welcome to the United World Paranormal Seekers

"Fecking ghost hunters again?" he grumbled. "Didn't I just get rid of you people a few weeks ago? Every time I turn around, here you come bothering me again."

He looked down at a stack of papers on the table and read the information on the top page. It was a schedule of events for the week. "Don't these morons have anything better to do with their time?" he exclaimed and scattered the papers all over the floor with a flick of his hand.

"Did you see that?" he heard someone say from behind him. He turned to see a woman with two men, all three of them wearing shirts with the words 'ghost hunter' scribbled across their chests.

The lady came over and walked right through him as he stood there with his arms folded.

"I just got a chill!" she announced to the others before pulling out a black box with little colored lights from her large 'I'd Rather Be Ghost Hunting' bag. "Is someone here? Give us a sign!

Can you please light up the box I am holding? All you have to do is touch it!"

Colin rolled his eyes. "I would rather shove it up your arse! Would that light it up?" he shouted into her ear. "How would that be for a sign?"

"I just heard a whisper!" the woman jumped up and down, squealing with excitement.

One of the men quickly rushed over and held up a smaller box with silver buttons. "Can you say something into my voice recorder? Just talk right into the end of it."

"Yes!" Colin leaned closer to the contraption in the man's hand. "You are all fecking idiots. Why don't you go do something useful with your lives instead of annoying the dead! Haven't you ever heard of allowing a soul to 'rest in peace'?"

The man clicked the recorder and played it back. They all heard it say, "Can you say something into my voice recorder? Just talk into the end of it—'dead'!"

"Dead? Do you know you are dead?" the man asked dramatically.

"Of course, I know, you dumb shite! Do you think I would hang around here with all of you willingly if I could be anywhere else? I swear, dealing with you fools is worse than being dead! Why don't you all just go away and leave me alone?"

Colin stormed out of the house, desperately needing to cool

his temper, producing a gusty breeze as he went. Standing on the walkway with his fists clenched in rage, some movement caught his eye, and he noticed someone standing close to his mother's grave. He traipsed up the hill, furious that anyone dared to go near her final resting place, but when he approached the spot, he stopped, and his anger slowly faded.

An attractive young woman stood before his mother's burial spot and had just finished pulling back the overgrown plants, clearing off his mother's headstone. It was something he had been wanting to do himself for years. While he could move little things when he concentrated, he could not do a job that big, and it was something that gnawed at him each day. She brushed the dirt from her hands and knees and started toward the loch. Watching her go, he waited before occupying the vacant spot in front of the now visible grave and silently paid his respects, touched and grateful beyond measure for the single rose that had been placed on his mother's stone in memoriam.

After looking over the schedule, Willow realized her services were not needed until the next day. She and Ronnie went into town, having some dinner at a pub before returning to the castle.

Exhausted from the trip when they returned, she stripped down to her t-shirt and climbed onto the bed. "Not the most comfortable thing I have ever laid on, but I suppose it will do," she murmured and pulled the bedspread over her, too tired to care if someone had been murdered on it. She shifted around a few times and had just gotten settled on her side when Ronnie decided to join her.

"Tired, baby?" he slipped into bed beside her and started to rub her bottom.

"Yes, I am," she replied and buried her face in her pillow, already half asleep.

"Don't worry, I will be quick so you can get some rest," he said and slid his hand under the covers, tugging unceremoniously at her underwear.

"I am not in the mood," she mumbled and swatted him away without even opening her eyes.

"Come on, Willow," he said, pressing against her from behind before moving to nibble on her earlobe. "I only need a couple of minutes, and you can go right back to sleep."

"A couple of minutes is all you EVER need," she muttered under her breath.

"Babe!" he whined.

"I said, not tonight, Ronnie!" she snapped. "It's been a long day, and I am exhausted from the trip. If you need it that badly, just go down the hall to the bathroom and handle it yourself."

"FINE!" he shouted angrily, threw back the covers, and pulled on his sweatpants. "I'm going downstairs." He stomped out of the room and slammed the door hard behind him.

"Perfect!" she said sleepily and waved him off. "Have fun

with yourself!"

Colin looked on with amusement and chuckled softly as he sat in a chair by the fireplace, enjoying the night's entertainment. He had been watching the rather odd couple all afternoon and had concluded he didn't care for the man called 'Ronnie' one bit. The sight of him being turned down flat by a woman, especially that one, pleased him more than he cared to admit. His gaze wandered back over to the bed, and he noticed the covers had fallen exactly right so that the woman, who the jackass had called by the name 'Willow', was partially exposed and her rather curvy backside was gloriously on display. Her long auburn-red hair angled her face perfectly and served to accent her creamy, porcelain skin, giving her the appearance of an angel sent straight down from Heaven. She was dressed only in a shirt and a pair of what they called, in this day and time 'panties'.

He didn't care what they called them; he only knew he liked them a great deal. Standing, he moved to the edge of the bed for a better perspective of the sleeping beauty. The ones she wore were black and appeared to be made with a thin strip of lace that went right between her plump, firm cheeks that had turned slightly pink from where Ronnie had touched her.

Biting his lip, he let out a resigned sigh and thought about how it would feel to use his teeth to tug at that fabric. God, he missed women! The worst thing about being dead was knowing you would never again feel the touch of a woman's body, and it was sheer torture, especially since he was doomed to roam in a place where couples visited to 'enjoy' each other all the time. Often, he would sneak a peek at their nocturnal activities, and it made him yearn for better days.

The woman shifted slightly, and the curve of her left breast came into full view. The top she wore was white and extremely thin, and the outline of her nipple stood out grandly.

Making himself comfortable, he stretched out on the bed next to her and propped up on one elbow to better partake of the lovely view. On a whim, he reached out his hand and used his finger to trace the outline of her upturned shoulder. While he was unable to feel anything himself, he was surprised to hear her sigh slightly in her sleep. Curious, he dropped his fingers down to the smallest part of her waist—and she let out a little groan as she snuggled in.

Wondering if she was reacting to him or something in her sleep, he let his hand glide down and over her hips and buttocks. He was amazed when she made a delightful sound and scooched her bottom back and closer to him as if to ask for more. Smirking, he leaned over and planted a light kiss on the back of her neck. Much to his surprise, she reached her hand back to feel for him, but she only felt emptiness. Suddenly, she rolled onto her back, then onto her left side, and lazily opened her eyes.

Willow was having a vivid dream…and what a marvelous dream it was! She was lying in bed in a castle in Scotland, beside a large hunk of a man with dark hair down to his waist and wearing an old-fashioned long kilt. The highlander was touching her in places, and in ways, Ronnie never did. She found her body responding, pleading for more.

The man lifted his eyebrows and smiled smugly as his gaze fell to her nipples; they had decided to stand at full attention in reaction to his sensual stroke.

She smiled back, blinked a few times, and sat straight up when she realized this was no dream. There happened to be a very real ghost staring lasciviously at her breasts.

"What the hell are you doing in my bed?" she shouted and pulled the sheet to cover herself.

Colin was clearly taken aback when she addressed him directly. He looked around to make sure there was no one else in the room she could be speaking to. "Wait, you can see me?" he raised up and asked, bemused. "You can actually see me? And hear me as well?"

She wagged her finger at him. "Who the fuck are you, and what are you doing in my bed?" she demanded.

"MY bed actually!" he corrected. "I am the Laird Colin MacLeod," he said and sat up. "How is it possible you can see me?"

"I see dead people," she replied. "You do know you are dead, right?" she asked as an afterthought.

"I sort of figured that one out on my own when I was able to look down at my own bloody body on the floor," he replied, dryly.

"Colin MacLeod?" she asked and scratched her head, thinking back to the story she heard upon their arrival. "Wait, are you the one who murdered your wife and brother? In this very bed?" She looked down, made a face, and quickly scrambled off.

He gracefully rolled off the edge of the mattress and onto his feet. "I did not murder them!" he retorted and went to stand by the fireplace. "I loved my little brother very much, and I did not care enough about my wife to go to the trouble of killing her!"

"That's not what the caretaker said!" she argued.

"Well, he was wrong!" he fired back. "How would he know anyway? It's not like he was there!"

She wrapped the sheet around her as another, more pressing, question popped into her head. She pointed downward. "Is this the actual bed they were murdered in?"

"Of course not!" He took a step toward it, scrunched up his face, and conducted a closer examination of the bedpost. "At least...I don't think it is?"

Willow dropped her head. "Jesus Christ! I was just sleeping in a bed where two people were murdered!"

Colin waved his hand dismissively. "Well, I'm fairly certain they have at least changed the mattress at some point over the years!"

Willow pulled the sheet tighter around her body before waddling over to the table that held the scotch. She poured a glass, drank it down, and stared back at him.

He motioned with his hands grandly at the chair for her to please sit.

She refilled her cup and moved to take the seat, watching him intently the entire time.

"Please, tell me how it is you can see me?" he asked earnestly. "No one has been able to see or communicate with me in well over four hundred years."

"I am what they call a 'medium'. I can see people who have passed, spirits who are stuck because of some unfinished business that must be handled before they can move on, or even ones who have already crossed over and simply choose to come back to reassure their loved ones they are well."

"You are a witch!" he exclaimed.

"No, I am not a witch. I believe in God and even manage to make it to church on most Sundays. I believe He gave me this ability to help people find peace and comfort when the death of their loved ones occur. I just happen to believe in some additional things, as well."

"That's all well and good for the living, but what of the dead who have been left behind?" Colin sat down on the edge of the bed and looked down. "I suppose He has forgotten about me."

Willow felt the sadness rolling off him and it bothered her immensely. "Or maybe that is why I am here?" she suggested. "They say the Lord works in mysterious ways and I have to tell you, a whole lot of crazy shit had to come together for me to end up here. Unfortunately, they weren't all good things."

He lifted his eyes to look at her. "You think you were sent here to help me, after all this time?"

She crossed her legs and pulled the sheet over her lap. "You never know, but since I am already here, I am certainly willing to give it a try. Why don't you start by telling me exactly what happened that night?"

Willow sipped her whiskey and listened, mindful not to interrupt as Colin explained about finding out his brother was in love with his wife, the plan to get them away to safety, the murders, and finally, the castle attack and his death.

"That's quite a story," she said when he was finished. Willow looked at him, puzzled. "You were just going to let your wife go off with your brother to be happy together? I expect any other man who found out his new bride was sleeping with his brother would have..."

"Murdered them?" he finished for her with a wry look on his face.

She bobbed her head around and winced.

He shrugged. "Yes, well, we would have all been miserable

if they had stayed, and it's not like I actually loved her. If our plan had worked, it would have given us all a chance to find a little peace in that lifetime."

Willow shook her head and appeared extremely confused. "I don't understand. You have done nothing that should keep you from moving on. As a matter of fact, you did everything right and then went above and beyond. Have you seen any other spirits while you are here?"

"None that would acknowledge me!"

"What's the very last thing you remember?" she asked.

He thought back. "My brother-in-law telling me the pain would be gone soon," he paused, "wait, there was something else. Finn said something about not wanting to see my sister upset, and then he called out some words I did not understand."

"Do you think it was a curse of some sort?" she questioned.

"I don't think so. He and I always got along exceptionally well, and he was the one who suggested I come up with a plan of deception for Sabina and Brody to be together."

Willow rubbed her eyes as the jet lag started to cloud her mind. "You know what? I need to give this some more thought when I can think a little clearer, and right now, I am beyond exhausted with the flight and the time difference."

"Of course!" Colin stood. "My deepest apologies! I was so elated when I discovered someone could see and hear me that it caused me to overstep and impose upon you. You need your rest, and I have rudely kept you from it. I will take my leave, and we can speak again when it is convenient for you. After all, it's not like I am going anywhere. I have nothing but time on my hands."

He started to fade out.

"Wait, before you go, I do have one question that is bugging the utter shit out of me," she said as she got out of the chair and stumbled over to the bed.

He waited for her query with a solemn expression on his face.

"If you are Scottish, why do you have an English accent?"

"Oh, that!" His face split into a wide grin. "My mother was from London, and she insisted we have tutors from there, much to my father's chagrin. She wanted us to sound more civilized." He stepped closer to her. "Thank you, by the way, for clearing off her grave and especially for leaving the rose. I used to visit her every day when I was alive. I maintained the garden personally, but I have slowly watched it deteriorate for over four hundred years. You were the first one to show any regard for it. Your kindness truly touched my heart. I am forever in your debt for that."

"It was my pleasure," she said with a yawn as she crawled onto the bed. As the side of her face flattened against a pillow and she hugged it tightly to her, she said, "Are you sure they changed this mattress?"

"Of course, I am," he lied and made a face as he looked again, not entirely sure if his answer was correct or not. That bed did look oddly familiar.

He glanced down at her, but she was already asleep. Colin moved back to the chair and found himself watching over her until that wretch Ronnie returned to the room in the middle of the night.

The man was drunk off his arse, and after removing his clothing, he climbed into bed and inched his way up behind Willow as close as he could.

Colin looked on angrily, as the man tried to shimmy off her underwear again, without her permission, and while she was out cold. That bastard was going to try to have his way with her whether she was willing or not. Colin became enraged at his audacity. No man had the right to force himself upon a woman who did not want him. He had more than his fair share of women when he was alive, but they were all wholly in desire of him, whether it had been for pleasure or coin.

He focused all his energy and went to stand over him. "Get away from her!" he ordered in his ear and laid an icy hand on the back of his neck.

Ronnie jumped straight up, falling off the side of the bed and looking over his shoulder fearfully. When he saw no one else was in the room, he gathered his clothes, pulled on his pants, and ran out of the room.

"Run away, you bastard!" muttered Colin under his breath. He went to check on Willow, and found her peacefully sleeping, blissfully unaware of what had just transpired. He smiled, lightly touched her face with the back of his hand and vanished.

Colin found himself in the downstairs library, which now housed a small bar for the guests. He would often hang around to take in the aroma of freshly poured whiskey since that was all he could still enjoy. William, the caretaker, liked to take a few nips over the course of the day, and would often hide out in there until a guest appeared at the desk to interrupt him. This room used to be the location of a large ornate carved desk, one that many MacLeod family discussions were held over and where he was officially deemed Laird by his father. Aenghus MacDonnell had used it as kindling when he burned all their bodies in a massive pile after the slaughter that day, a memory that would never be erased from his mind. Colin leaned over a glass on the counter as one of the pesky ghost hunter men left his drink unattended to go take a piss.

He smiled and waved his hand over it so the smell would waft upwards. He sighed and was about to leave when he noticed Ronnie had come into the room. Colin scowled at him as he walked by and went to join a young woman on the sofa. Curiosity got the better of him and he moved to stand by the fireplace to watch them, eavesdropping on their conversation.

The woman had short pink hair, along with some sort of metal in her nose and, when she laughed, she exposed what appeared to be a nail that went through her tongue. "What the devil is that?" he asked, leaning in for a closer look. He slipped in, planted himself between them on the couch, and turned his attention to her piercing. "Were you being punished for something? Was it for not offering a confession or gossiping too much?" he asked as he scrunched up his face. "I must say, that looks extremely painful."

"Jade, I don't think I have ever met anyone with an actual tongue ring before." Ronnie put his arm along the back of the couch.

"Yeah, I just got it pierced a few months ago," she smiled and crossed her legs.

"You did that on purpose?" asked Colin. "Why would anyone deform themselves in such a manner?"

Jade scooted closer to Ronnie. "I got it for my ex-boyfriend because he insisted it would make things hotter in the bedroom, but he's not around anymore. We broke up last week and now, here I am, all alone." The woman poked out her lips in a pouty manner.

"What man would want a woman to do that for him?" Colin started to feel a bit closed in.

Ronnie and the pink-haired one were inching closer to each other.

Ronnie bit his lip. "Explain to me again what it's good for."

Jade moved her hand through Colin to touch Ronnie on the

leg and whispered. "Well, he said after I got it, I gave him the best head he had ever had in his entire life."

"Head?" Colin stroked his chin, trying to figure out what she meant. "How could she give him a head?"

Just then, Jade ran her hand up the inside of Ronnie's inner thigh, rubbing his crotch while licking her lips wantonly. She stuck out her tongue and slowly moved it up and down as her eyes fell to his growing bulge.

"Oh! OH!" exclaimed Colin, watching her actions, and it dawned on him what she was referring to. "How does that make it better? I wonder!" he cocked his head to the side, pondering the question as he slowly faded away.

3

CHAPTER THREE

Willow slept in late the next morning and found herself alone when she woke up. Having to wait to use the shower of their shared bathroom situation, she barely made it in time for her first group reading that afternoon where she answered question after question for over an hour. She was pleasantly amused to see Colin sitting among the participants in a chair at the very back, paying close attention to each interaction. When the reading was over, she waited for the room to clear and walked back to take the seat next to him.

"What did you think?" she asked.

He smiled. "I think you are exceptionally good at what you do. Everyone here who had questions for, and about, their loved ones, seemed more content after your answers, and that is a good thing." Colin looked down and his mood became serious. "I do have a question of my own for you, though."

"What is it?"

He rubbed his chin. "Do you actually see the people who have passed over that you speak to? I ask because I did not see another spirit the entire time this was going on."

Willow shook her head. "Not today. Sometimes, they do appear in front of me, and at inopportune times, like when I am in the bathroom or otherwise engaged," she rolled her eyes, "but more often than not, the ones who have crossed over just sort of whisper in my ear. I only repeat the message they give me to their loved ones."

He turned to face her. "But how do you get them to come to you to begin with? How do you call for them?"

"I don't. I think they just follow their family members around and wait until they can get the attention of someone who can see or hear them. I believe most of these 'hauntings' people experience are loved ones just trying to reach out."

He looked crestfallen. "So, there is no way to ask for someone specifically to come through?"

Willow bobbed her head back and forth. "There are people who sometimes use spirit boards to do that. I for one don't, because you can never be sure who, or what, is actually coming through. People who don't know what they're doing can open portals to other places and bring in nasty, unwanted guests that are difficult to get rid of and tend to wreak havoc while they are here. Why do you ask?"

"I was simply curious. Our conversation last night made me wonder about my own family and even more about the words my brother-in-law, Finn, spoke to me before I died. I thought if there was a way to summon him, perhaps he could answer some questions about why I am trapped here."

As people began to wander back into the room, Colin hung his head sadly and slowly faded out.

"Well, goodbye to you too," she said dryly. "Buddy, you give a whole new meaning to the term 'being ghosted'."

Willow looked up to see the old man from check-in making his way in her direction. "The organizer just called. He asked me to pass along word there would be a 'meet-and-greet' and some other event this evening at around 11 pm. Ye are expected to attend them both."

"Thank you," she said and held up her finger. "Exactly who IS the organizer of this whole thing? I don't believe anyone has said."

The old man shrugged and turned to shuffle away. "I don't ask, and I don't want to know. All I care about is their money."

"Can't beat these Scottish men and their charm," she muttered sarcastically to herself.

Willow stood up. Looking around, it occurred to her she had not seen Ronnie that morning. She searched the house and grounds to no avail and decided he was probably still sulking from last night when she turned him down. "I suppose I should make it up to him," she sighed and started back to their room to wait for him.

As she passed by the kitchen, she caught a glimpse of something out of the corner of her eye. Stopping abruptly, she took several steps backward until she had a full view of what was happening.

Several women moved back and forth in the room, which had transformed from an empty kitchen into a bustling setting full of busy people in long gowns—some cooked over the large fireplace, others chopped vegetables, and a few kneaded bread doughs. One older lady was obviously in charge and moved unhurriedly as she supervised the others. Walking slowly over to a chair, she produced a bottle and turned it up to take a long swig. No sound came from them, but they all acted as if they were happily chatting away while they worked.

She felt Colin's presence beside her. The pair watched solemnly in silence as the scene unfolded before them.

"That's Molly with the bottle," he finally whispered. "She was like a mother to us after our own mother died and that woman, well, she was a wise soul cut from a vastly different cloth. I loved her very much. I have tried to speak to her and the others many times, but they never acknowledge me, acting as if they do not see or hear me."

"Because they don't," she said, softly and gently. "It is what we call a 'residual haunting'. Sometimes, for reasons we don't understand, stone walls and floors like the ones here absorb the energy from everyday events and it creates an impression. Occasionally, that energy is released back into the world and the scene is replayed."

"So, they are not trapped here like me?"

"No. As a matter of fact, other than the spirits who have come along with the people in the paranormal group, so far, you are the only one I have seen here."

The event slowly faded and returned to the present time. Willow started toward the hall and the staircase while they continued to speak. "The beeps and flashing lights these people are getting on their equipment are merely coming from their loved ones trying to connect. Sometimes, it even comes from their imaginations because they want to believe in it so badly. Those people are so desperate to make some sort of contact with the other side that it makes their minds play tricks on them. It's fairly peaceful here in this house—well, other than you, that is."

"It is good to know they are not suffering," he said and slowly dissipated.

Willow sighed as she absorbed the weight of his loneliness. She continued up the staircase.

Colin looked out over the loch, his mind processing the fact he was the only one who did not cross over that day. Something held him here, but he could not for the life of him figure out what it was. Deciding to pay his mother's grave a visit to clear his head, he heard rather unusual noises coming from a group of trees as he neared the house. Curiosity got the better of him, and he moved closer for a better look.

Ronnie was there, with his trousers down around his ankles and his scrawny, bare arse in the air. He was on his knees, having his way with the pink-haired woman, Jade, taking her from behind, the way a stray dog takes a bitch in heat. He finished in an exceptionally short amount of time, smacked her on the behind, and stood to pull up his pants.

"Will I see you later?" she asked, climbing to her feet and adjusting her noticeably short skirt, the one he had merely shoved up around her waist for the act.

"Count on it!" He laughed and pulled off the sheath he had used, tossed it into the woods, and zipped up his pants. "I will come to your room later, and you can show me how that tongue ring works." Ronnie left her there alone and started for the house.

"You fecking bastard!" exclaimed Colin.

Willow lay across the bed waiting for Ronnie, staring up at the ceiling and letting her thoughts drift to Colin's situation. She couldn't get his predicament off her mind—or him for that matter. He may have been a ghost, but even death could not conceal his handsome, rugged face, those broad, muscular shoulders, or the way he made a long kilt look. That man was the stuff unforgettable dreams were made of—the kind you never wanted to wake from and left your body feeling all the right things in all the best places.

"Focus!" she said to herself and tapped her head with both palms. "What can possibly be holding him here?" He hadn't done anyone wrong, committed some atrocious murder, or been just a horrible person in general, at least she didn't think he had. She only had his word to go on, and he HAD been there for over four hundred years, which is a great deal of time to look back over your life and to see everything in a different light. Maybe he hadn't been a good person after all, and time had just made him forget that little fact. She blew out a deep breath. "Who knows?"

The rattle of the doorknob broke her concentration, and she looked over to see Ronnie come into the room.

"Where have you been?" she asked.

"Oh, just out and about," he said curtly, sat down on the edge of the bed, and took off his shoes.

She made a face behind his back and forced herself to apologize. "I'm sorry about last night. I was just tired and jet-lagged. This place is sort of getting to me."

"You can make it up to me, baby," he smirked and twisted around to place his hand on her thigh. "You WERE kind of harsh last night," he pretended to pout. Ronnie shucked off his shirt, moved across the bed, and rolled her underneath him before she knew what was happening. Quickly unfastening her jeans, he started to work them down over her hips.

"You know, foreplay is a thing, and you at least used to kiss me," she complained with her arms stretched above her head and looking off to the side.

"I just want you so badly, and I can't wait baby," he replied as he yanked the jeans off, and chucked them over his shoulder, frowning when he realized he didn't get her panties as well.

Willow rolled her eyes and was just about to remove them herself, resigned to the fact Ronnie did EVERYTHING half-assed when Colin's face suddenly appeared over his right shoulder. His expression was judgmental as if he were critiquing Ronnie's disappointing seduction technique.

"What are you doing?" she shouted.

"Isn't it obvious?" answered an annoyed Ronnie as he fumbled with his pants, unable to get his belt buckle loose. "Just give me a minute. I've almost got it!"

Willow's eyes widened as she mouthed 'go away' to Colin.

Colin stepped to the side and smugly looked down at the still struggling Ronnie. "You don't have such issues with kilts."

Willow nudged her head to the side to indicate he should leave.

Colin stretched out his arms in front of him, fake yawned, and casually mentioned, "The least he could do is go wash himself considering I saw him in the woods less than an hour ago, 'dipping his wick' into that dreadful ghost-hunting woman with the metal points sticking out of her face."

"What?" she shrieked and scooched back against the headboard.

"What?" demanded Ronnie, as he finally got his belt loose, unzipped his pants, and crawled up to her. "What's wrong?" he asked when he noticed she was focused on something over his shoulder. He looked behind him. "There's nothing there!" he said, annoyed. "Come on, baby," and he pulled his erection free, not bothering to take off his pants completely, only pushing them down over his hips a bit.

"That's unfortunate and rather unimpressive," remarked Colin disapprovingly when he caught a glimpse of Ronnie's modest member. "You know, Scottish men don't have that problem either."

"Did you just fuck someone else in the woods?" demanded Willow.

"No! Why would you think such a thing?" He leaned in for a kiss on the lips to placate her.

"He is waiting for you to go to sleep so he can go to her room and do it again later tonight. He wants to find out how that nail through her tongue feels when she is giving him— what did she call it—a head?" Colin propped his elbow on the bureau and scratched his chin. "I still haven't quite figured out what the term means."

Willow shoved Ronnie's face away with her hand and leapt off the bed. "You were just screwing another woman, and you plan on seeing her later to get a blowjob?"

Colin folded his arms and mouthed to himself, "Blowjob?" He looked down as if giving something a great deal of thought. "AH! THAT!" he nodded when the term finally made sense.

"Baby, I don't know what you are talking about! Why do you think I would do something like that to you? You know I love you!"

She pointed in Colin's direction. "Because HE told me!"

Colin smiled and waved.

"Who are you talking about?" screamed Ronnie. "There's no one there!"

Colin narrowed his eyes and concentrated on the empty scotch bottle on the nightstand. He waved his hand sharply, making it fly, and hit Ronnie square on the back of the head. His face went pale when he turned and saw no one was behind him. He rubbed the back of his head. "Who did that?"

Willow folded her arms and moved to Colin's side. "The Laird of the castle is not pleased with you, and we BOTH want you out of here! NOW!"

Colin pursed his lips and waved his finger in a circle. "Tell him if he does not leave my castle this minute, I will—umm—"

Willow lifted her finger in the air as she interrupted him. "I've got this!"

Colin held out both hands. "Please, be my guest!"

"The Laird says if you don't leave this property this minute, you will die a horrific death in your sleep the way two others who royally pissed him off did in this very room."

Colin moved over to Ronnie and leaned close to his ear. "BOO!"

Ronnie shrieked like a little girl and made a beeline for the door. He fell face forward and banged his forehead into the doorknob, as he got tangled up in his pants, which had fallen around his ankles. He wiped his face, looked down at the blood on his hand, and screamed again. Somehow managing to open the door, he crawled out into the hall where a group of paranormal investigators were taking pictures.

They looked at him oddly, turned their cameras on him, and started snapping away.

Willow and Colin watched from the doorway as Ronnie attempted to gather his clothing, along with what was left of his dignity, and rushed away from the scene as fast as he could. Willow slammed the door closed, went back into the room, and collapsed on the bed. "I can't believe that bastard cheated on me," she muttered and covered her face with her hands. "Not only have I given him a place to live, but I have been financially supporting that son-of-a-bitch for the past six months while my business has been going under." She curled on her side and a few angry tears slipped down her cheek. "How could I be such an idiot?"

"You are far from being an idiot," he assured, "and you are better off without him!" Colin sat down on the edge of the bed. "I'm sorry," he said sincerely, feeling guilty for being the one who broke the news. "I didn't want to upset you, but I thought you needed to know he was being unfaithful to you. There is nothing worse than having someone you think you can trust betray you in such a way."

"I did need to know," she sniffled, "but it doesn't make it hurt any less."

"Oh lass, he was not good enough for you. You deserve a man who is solely devoted to you and someone who will satisfy you in bed."

She blinked, raised up, and cut him a look. "What makes you think he didn't satisfy me in bed?"

"Oh, come on!" he scoffed. "You said yourself last night he only lasted a couple of minutes, and I did just see what he had to work with. What well-tended woman could be satisfied with THAT?"

She narrowed her eyes at him. "How do you know what I said to him last night?"

He winced. "I may have overheard?"

Willow sat up. "So, you have been hanging around in my room and watching what I do?" She folded her arms over her breasts and subconsciously covered herself. "Have you seen me while I was undressed?"

He attempted to look innocent but failed miserably.

Her mouth flew open in disbelief.

"It's not like I have never seen a naked woman before," he offered.

Willow pulled the pillow from behind her head and threw it at, or rather, through him. "GET OUT!" she shouted.

"Oh, come on, Willow!" he pleaded and flashed a sexy smile. "Would you be less cross with me if I told you that you have the most beautiful, round, plump arse I have seen in over four hundred years?"

"OUT!" she growled.

He winked and faded away.

"Plump arse!" she mocked scornfully. "How dare he say my arse is 'plump'? Who even uses that word anymore?" Willow laid back down, pulled another pillow over her face, and screamed into it as she flailed her legs. "A faithless leech and a ghost who is a peeping Tom—can this trip get any worse?"

Willow tossed the pillow to the floor and noticed one of Ronnie's shirts on the bureau.

"Oh, HELL no!" She got up, slipped on her jeans, and gathered his items. Balling up his clothes, she stuffed them into his suitcase, then grabbed his toiletry bag and tossed it on top. As another wave of anger washed over her, she took out his toothbrush, looked around, and marched over to the slightly opened window. Willow then used it to scrub out a spot of black mildew on the outside windowsill. She smiled devilishly when she saw a spot of bird poop on the pane as well and reached up to add it into the mix. Triumphantly, she stuffed it back into his bag, zipped his suitcase, and hauled it downstairs. She smacked the service bell on the desk until someone appeared.

A pleasant, slim middle-aged woman with a glass of scotch in her hand popped her head in. "Oh, hello! Did ye need something, dear?" she asked when she appeared.

"You aren't the gentleman from earlier," noted Willow.

"The cranky one? Oh, that's William. I sent him off for a nap because the guests were complaining he was putting his head down on the desk, pretending to be dead, and shouting at folks when they tried to check on him."

Willow grinned. "What was he saying to them?"

"Apparently, he would wait for one to poke him, then jump and say, "Boo! Ye found your ghost, now get the hell out and don't ask for a refund!"

Willow laughed aloud. "I have to say, William is starting to grow on me."

"Well, ye would be the only one! I am Marion, by the way. What can I do for ye?"

"Yes!" she rolled the bag over to her. "You can have this sent up to the room of whatever woman my cheating-ass boyfriend was 'doing' in the woods earlier before he came back and tried to have sex with me. He is all hers!"

"Men are disgusting pigs!" scoffed Marion. "But we do need them for one or two things, don't we?"

Willow unzipped one of the side pockets. "Just so he doesn't have to speak to me anymore, here is his passport," and she placed it on the desk. "Although, I should probably get home before he does so I can change the locks at my apartment and dump the rest of his shit in the garbage chute."

Marion looked down at it, then back up at Willow. She picked up the passport and dropped it into her glass. "Oh, this passport? The one that accidentally fell into my drink. Well, it's a shame I am so clumsy."

Marion waved her hand and motioned for Willow to follow her into the library and over to the fireplace. She leaned down, let the corner of the small book catch fire, and burn a few seconds before she dropped it onto the hearth and stomped it out with the toe of her high heel shoe.

"Ye have to be careful around these damn candles when the breeze blows through these drafty old places," she smirked, before she picked it up, still smoldering, and dropped it back in the glass. "That should buy ye some time."

"Marion, I think you are my new favorite person!" Willow grinned.

Marion set the glass on the mantle. "It looks like I need a fresh drink. Care to join me?"

"I would love to! I am Willow by the way."

"Ye are the medium, aren't ye?" asked Marion as she went to the small bar and poured two glasses.

"That's me," she replied, accepting the glass gratefully, and moving to sit down on a leather sofa.

"I am guessing ye are not a psychic, as well, if ye didn't see what the cheating bastard was doing."

"No, I am afraid I only see dead people, but it WAS a ghost who ratted him out."

"Well, that sounds like an interesting story I would love to hear more about at some point!" Marion sat down next to her, crossed her legs, and sipped her glass. "So are ye ready for tonight?"

"The meet-and-greet? I guess?"

"Meet-and-greet?" Marion appeared confused. "Oh no! Didn't anyone tell ye what today is?"

Willow shook her head.

"Today is the anniversary of the battle and the deaths here at the castle. The organizer has planned a special ghost hunting session at midnight."

"What?" Willow downed her drink. "William left out that little part."

"He would!" she grumbled. "Well, it should be interesting nonetheless," said Marion just before she heard the bell ring, alerting her to someone at the desk. She stood. "Excuse me, but duty calls. Stay as long as ye like and help yourself to anything ye like from the bar."

"Thanks for everything!" said Willow as she watched her go.

Grabbing a full bottle from behind the counter, she headed up to her room.

Half an hour later, Willow lay across the bed, drunk, and giggling to herself.

"May I please come in?" called Colin, seemingly from the air. "If you notice, I am politely asking permission to enter the room. I can't exactly knock."

"What do you want?" she groaned.

Colin's head appeared first. He looked down at her, noticed her disheveled appearance, along with the half-empty bottle, and frowned as the rest of him slowly formed. "I am guessing you are not much of a drinker."

"I am today! It's not every day you get cheated on by your sleazy boyfriend and stalked by a depraved ghost in a rundown castle in Scotland."

He closed his eyes. "Please accept my sincerest apologies. I am not accustomed to being seen and heard by other people and, at that time, I was completely unaware you could communicate with me."

"So, you just spy on unsuspecting women in their bedrooms? Do you watch people when they are having sex too?" she asked.

"Not intentionally," he responded carefully and sat down next to her, "but I am not going to lie. If I see it occurring, I normally do not look away. There is so little to do in the afterlife, and I admit, I get bored easily."

"Do you get off on watching people?" she asked. "Can the dead even get horny? I mean, I know you can't get a hard on because technically you don't have a body part to get hard—" she mused and scratched her head, confused by her own questions. "Do you still get the urge to—you know —do the deed?"

"Dear Lord, you are exceptionally drunk, aren't you!" he declared before he lay back and stretched out next to her. "To answer your question, when I see a beautiful woman, yes, I do feel a certain longing that stirs within me but acting on it is another issue altogether. In this form, I am entirely harmless, and the women of this castle are completely safe from my impulses. I do, however, miss the physical pleasures of the flesh very much."

Willow waved her finger around in the air. "Speaking of spying on people, I have a question. This room is rather secluded at the end of the hall, so how did Nahla see Brody and Sabina together?"

"Oh! She snuck into the secret room and thought she was going to see me with Sabina doing 'what couples do'. When she saw Brody instead, she became upset, terrified their father would kill them both, force her to marry me, and proceeded to react rashly."

"There's a secret room?" she exclaimed excitedly. "Where? Show me!"

Colin raised on his elbow and pointed to the far wall. "The peephole is still over there, but the room itself was sealed off years ago."

She rolled onto her side to face him and whispered, "Why is there a secret room again?"

"This bedchamber was used specifically for wedding nights. Families and clergy could watch the marriage be consummated so there was no doubt, and no annulment could be demanded."

"No way!" She sat up. "They watched you have sex on your honeymoon? What kind of perverts do something like that?"

He folded his hands behind his head. "My father, her father, and the priest along with a few more witnesses from both families."

"So, the apple didn't fall far from the tree? You inherited your perversion from your father's side," she said dryly.

He cut her a sharp look.

"How fucked up is that?" she asked and fell back on the bed. "Tell me, why did Sabina agree to marry you to begin with if she loved Brody?"

"She had no choice in the matter. Women had little, if any, say in such things back then. Her father told her if she didn't marry me and bed me the wedding night, he would slit her throat and marry me off to Nahla."

"The thirteen-year-old? Who would do something like that to their own daughter? What a lousy piece-of-shit father! How come he is not the one stuck between Heaven and Hell?"

"Indeed!" he agreed. "I am guessing your father would never have done something so heinous to you?"

"I wouldn't know," she muttered. "I have never met the man."

"You don't know who your father is?"

She shook her head. "My mother never said one word about him. I asked once when I was a kid, but she became so upset I never brought it up again. It doesn't matter. She busted her ass to be both parents to me, and she was perfect."

"Children should know their fathers," he said, softly. "And fathers should always be there to protect and provide for their children, no matter what."

"I don't think I would have survived living back in your time period," she commented as she rolled over on her stomach and tried to change the subject. "Arranged marriages, people watching you fuck on your wedding night, no toilets or air conditioning... nope, not the life for me!"

Colin grinned. "Personally, I think you would have made it pretty interesting."

"Why didn't you tell me today was the anniversary of what

happened?" she asked, out of the blue.

"It doesn't serve any purpose. Besides, I will be reminded soon enough."

"What do you mean by that?"

"Each year, the—what did you call it—the 'residual energy' replays the battle in the main hall just at midnight and, each year, I watch my family and friends get slaughtered all over again. It is not a day I look forward to."

She pushed up on her arms. "Lucky for you, I am here." She went to slap him on the upper arm, but her right hand went through him. She tried again with her left and again with her right but ended up looking more like a kitten batting at an imaginary toy.

"Ghost! Remember?" he reminded.

"Oh, yeah that's right," she said. "I forgot for a moment."

He shook his head and looked perplexed. "I don't understand what you mean by 'you being here'. What difference would it make?"

"A pair of fresh eyes watching your last moments? Maybe I can see what happened to prevent you from moving on?"

"You think it's possible?"

She fell face down. "Anything is possible, and it's worth a try. Wake me up in time," she yawned and passed out.

Colin smiled to himself. He rolled onto his side and hesitated before he placed his hand on the curve of her back. She responded with a sigh and pressed back against the space where his hand was.

"Oh aye, lass. I do feel something. Something I have never felt before, and I am in Hell all over again knowing I can never share it with you," he whispered. She started to snore lightly, and he continued to rest his hand there as he watched her sleep.

4

CHAPTER FOUR

Willow slept through the meet-and-greet, as well as the beginning of the 'special hunt'. She was awakened at about 11:45 pm by the sound of Colin's voice shouting in her ear.

"I'm up!" she groaned.

"Oh good, I thought you might be dead for a moment," he said dryly. "Come on, it's time."

She sat up, pushed the hair from her eyes, and slowly moved from the bed, still groggy. Grabbing a bottle of water from the table, she followed him downstairs. When they got to the main hall, the room was packed full of investigators.

"Fucking ghost hunters!" she mumbled to herself, her words inspiring him to conceal a smirk behind his hand.

"We need to get rid of them so you can see the full picture when it happens," he pointed out.

"I got this," she grumbled and sighed. She walked to the middle of the room, raised her hand to her temple, and stated loudly, rather overdramatically, "Oh! What is that you say spirits from the other side? There's a midnight gathering of all the ghosts of the castle down by the loch? You have a message about the murders you wish to convey?" She looked around. "The victims of the murders want to be heard on this most sacred of nights, and they want to tell you what happened. You all should go quickly before they fade away for another whole year—blah, blah, blah. Go! Hurry before it is too late and don't forget your equipment! You wouldn't want to miss anything!"

The entire room cleared in less than three minutes.

"Nice work!" he said, rather impressed.

"I'm learning how to work a crowd," she replied and took a sip of her water.

As a nearby clock struck midnight, the room slowly shifted and transformed into something she was not prepared for. What she saw, horrified and astounded her all at the same time.

The entire main hall was completely filled with armed men locked in a tragic battle to the death, knee-deep in blood, bodies, and gore. One man ran his sword through the back of the one Colin called Molly, the poor woman merely trying to flee the carnage. Her face contorted in agony and shock as she staggered forward, but when Willow instinctively reached out, her hands filled with nothingness.

Willow found herself overcome with the woman's extreme fear. Shaking it off, she turned her attention back to the fight, only to witness more men being cut down and their blood painting the walls until, finally, no MacLeod was left standing. She found herself submerged in the deluge of intense sensations felt on that day and stopped to lean over with her hands on her knees to catch her breath.

"Are you alright?" Colin asked, his face full of worry.

She nodded. "Where are you during all of this?"

He pointed. "Over there by the fireplace."

She gulped in as much air as she possibly could with the heavy atmosphere making it more difficult to breathe and forced herself to move across the room, even though it felt like she was trudging through heavy mud. Finally, she laid eyes upon him. The Laird was lying in a pool of his own blood, pale, and on the verge of death. The sight brought her an immense amount of pain; her eyes welled with tears as she was overcome with emotion.

"I didn't suffer. I was not afraid to meet my maker," he whispered in her ear, wanting desperately to have the ability to wipe away the wetness spilling down her cheeks. "Please don't weep for me. It breaks my heart to see you cry."

"Liar!" she sniffled. "I can feel exactly what you felt. You were in excruciating pain and terrified beyond belief."

They watched together as Finn appeared from seemingly out of nowhere. He stepped through the sea of bodies and made his way over to his brother-in-law. Finn knelt and spoke some words to Colin; they only knew because his lips were moving, but no sound came from him.

Willow watched intently as Colin's hand slipped from Finn's grip and his soul departed his body...

—and then something rather bizarre and unworldly occurred—Finn turned, looked her directly in the eye, and spoke the words,

"To one who beholds what others cannot see,

I send forth this call across time and sea,

With a kiss that touches no mortal lips,

A scale from the past will soon be tipped,

State your desire plain and clear,

For the King of Fae and Fates to hear,

Your heart will help to lead the way,

And bring about a better day."

They stared in disbelief as the scene slowly faded from view before Willow turned to look at Colin.

"You saw and heard that too, right?"

Colin slowly nodded as he gawked at the now empty spot on the floor, bewildered and lost in his thoughts. "That has never happened before. He has always held my hand and vanished with the rest of the scene. No words have been spoken aloud since that fateful day."

Willow staggered a bit, which brought him back to his

senses. "Are you feeling unwell?" he asked, concerned. "What can I do?"

"I just need to sit down for a minute," she said, drained as she moved to a chair. "I don't usually feel what the dead feel in their final moments. I guess it took a lot out of me."

She leaned her head forward into her hands. Colin dropped to his knees before her, unable to do anything else. "So, you have never heard those words before?" she asked.

He shook his head. "No, never! Truthfully, I don't think they were meant for me. It was clear he was looking at, and speaking directly, to you."

"But you said none of them have ever acknowledged you."

He sighed. "They haven't, but again, he was reacting to you and not me. My spirit had already departed my body by then. This doesn't make any sense. What is different this time?"

Willow groaned as a wave of dizziness and nausea overcame her.

"You need to lie down," he declared with a troubled expression on his face. "Can you make it upstairs or do I need to get someone to help you?"

"How are you going to do that?" she asked, sarcastically.

Scratching his head, he frowned. "I am sure I can figure out something. I am a very resourceful spirit!"

"I'll manage," she replied and slowly stood. Wobbling slightly, he reached out for her arm. She looked down at his hand

and back up at him peculiarly when she realized she had actually felt his touch. After slowly making her way up to the room, she crawled into bed and flopped over on her back. "What's a 'Fae'?" she inquired.

Colin sat down on the foot of the bed. "An old being with magical powers who likes to meddle in the affairs of mankind. Our father would tell us stories of their adventures. Some of them liked people and would help them, like house brownies, while others liked to play cruel tricks and harm anyone they encountered, such as the Ghillie Dhu, but I can't say I have ever seen one. I think they were mostly stories to frighten children and keep them out of mischief."

"Like fairy tales?" she asked.

"Exactly!"

She thought back. "Finn said to state your desire to the King of Fae and Fates. How would one go about doing such a thing?"

"Call out to a creature who doesn't exist?" He shrugged. "What difference does it make if he's not real?"

Willow sat up and pulled her knees to her chest. "If I have learned one thing in this world, it is there is far more out there than we know or understand. For instance, most people don't sit around talking to depraved ghosts, yet here we are."

"I am not depraved!" he snapped. "I just have the healthy curiosity of any man. Besides," his tone softened, "I appreciate being able to see and speak with a beautiful and intelligent woman."

"You think I am 'beautiful'?" she teased with a gleam in her eye.

He smiled sweetly. "My dear, Willow, you are the most enchanting, desirable woman to pass through these doors in four hundred years. Believe me, I should know."

Willow tucked a strand of loose hair behind her ear and blushed. "Now you are just blowing smoke up my ass."

He blinked hard seemingly confused. "I would never blow smoke up your arse, whatever that means." Colin shifted closer. "And I can think of a hundred better things to do with an arse as magnificent as yours that would be a great deal more pleasurable for both of us."

Willow sighed as she stared at him and a few of those 'things' popped into her mind. It was just her luck, the hottest thing she had ever laid eyes on was sitting in front of her, gazing at her adoringly, and making suggestive comments. He also happened to be completely unattainable because he was a ghost.

He moved even closer to her. "If you are insinuating I am just saying things to flatter you, then you would be dead wrong. I don't know why, but for some inexplicable reason, I am drawn to you. God help me, I find myself having feelings for you I did not know I could have."

"Maybe it is because I am the only woman you have had a conversation with in four hundred years," she teased.

He bent his head slightly and leaned to whisper in her ear. "If you were only able to feel my touch, I would leave you with no doubt of my affection and desire for you."

Willow let out an audible squeak when she felt the warmth of his breath on her neck, sending a jolt down her spine, igniting a physical desire from within. Suddenly, she wanted him more than life itself. She closed her eyes and muttered, "If the King of Fae and Fate is real, I hope he hears these words... there is nothing I want more in this world than to feel what you feel for me."

She inhaled, surprised to catch a faint whiff of musk before sensing the movement of his face along the nape of her neck and back down the side of her cheek. Willow moaned when she felt the gentle press of his sultry, soft, and very solid lips against hers. A surge of peculiar energy ran down the entire length of her body, causing her to feel strange, as if her entire being were spinning out of control. She fell backward onto the bed, dizzy, but forced her eyes to remain open, her gaze locked on his. Colin towered over her, a distraught appearance on his face. "Willow! What's happening?" was the last thing she heard before everything   went   black.

5

CHAPTER FIVE

Willow was awakened the next morning by the warm, bright beams of sunlight streaming through the windowpanes. After losing a battle with the tangled hair covering her face, she pressed her palms to her eyes, rolled over, and groaned. Her head pounded, her mouth was painfully dry, and she felt a little nauseous, probably from the half bottle of scotch she had before Colin woke her for the midnight event. She pulled the covers over her head and pondered the events from the previous night. Did he really kiss her, or was it just a wistful dream of something which could never be? She didn't remember anything more, so maybe she imagined it after all. A glance down at her watch brought her back to the moment. "Shit! SHIT!" She had to give a reading in five minutes, so she fought back the covers and tossed her feet over the side. Wiping the sleep from her eyes, she looked around and blinked…then blinked again to be certain of what she was seeing.

"Whose room am I in?" she asked aloud.

This layout looked much like hers, but the bed covering was green, with tied-back curtains attached around it, enclosing it.

The furniture was also different, not to mention, much nicer than what was in her suite.

"Colin?" she called out, but there was no response. He was probably off somewhere scaring some of the ghost hunters for his own personal amusement, or maybe he was torturing Ronnie. The thought pleased her and brought a smile to her face.

Willow got up and went to the door. Thankfully, she had fallen asleep in her clothes, so at least she already had on jeans and a T-shirt, even if they did reek of sweat and alcohol. Willow gently pulled the door open and stepped into the hall. She turned to go in the direction of her room but realized there was nowhere to go because she was already there. Confused, she went to go back inside but, when she did, she stepped on something sharp on the floor that pierced her bare foot. "OW!" She hopped around for a minute as she looked around. Utterly confused by her whereabouts, she simply brushed off the blood with her hand. "This can't be right!" she said as she inspected the room. The design was the same, but all the furnishings had been switched out. "Colin!" she called out again louder only much more demanding and still received no response. "Damn it! Where the hell are you when I need you?"

She went back into the hall and started toward the stairs but was stopped by an older woman.

"Ah, here ye are!" she exclaimed as she firmly took her by the arm. "We have been looking all over for ye. Yer expected ye know!"

Willow frowned. "I am not that late!"

"Ye still need to get cleaned up," the old woman said. "And what are ye wearing? Ye are dressed like a man!"

Willow scrunched up her face, annoyed. "I am sorry my personal style isn't good enough for you," she mumbled, taking note of the older woman's longer dress.

"No matter!" said the woman, pulling her into a small room with a fireplace and a large metal tub filled with steaming hot water. "Ye can get washed up in here."

Willow looked over at the tub and grinned. "Someone has been holding out on me. The bathroom I have only has a shower."

The woman looked at her oddly and started to tug at her shirt.

"What are you doing?" asked Willow and shooed her away, aggravated by her impolite disregard of personal space.

"Helping ye wash, ye daft girl," she grumbled. "Ye can't take a bath in yer clothes."

"I can manage to undress all by myself. I have been doing it since I was five," she said and yanked down the hem of her shirt.

"Don't go getting uppity on me girl just because ye think ye are hot shite in the Laird's bed. It's not like ye are the only one who has ever been in his room. Yer nothing special, just another warm body to fill a space."

Willow turned to her. "I don't believe I got your name."

"I am Molly," said the old woman as she hung a robe on the

hook. "Now, take yer clothes off, and make yerself fit to be seen. When ye are done, just put this on, and wait for me. I will get ye some decent clothes to have for later."

Willow huffed when she realized this was a battle she wasn't going to win. Besides, the sight of the tub was just a little too inviting.

"Alright, Molly, I will do as you say, but just because I want to take a bath."

Molly scoffed and mumbled a few incoherent words on her way out.

Once she was gone, Willow stripped off her clothes, climbed in, and sank slowly until her head was the only thing showing above the water. "I think I have died and gone to Heaven," she said as she located a wonderful lavender soap and scrubbed down from head to toe. After soaking for a good little while, the door flew wide open, and Molly returned.

"Do you mind?" Willow shouted and covered her breasts with her hands.

Molly waved her off. "It's not like I haven't seen tits before. I've got two of my own after all." The older woman closed the door. "Although, yers sit much higher than mine. I used to have nice ones like that, ye know, but time is not kind to our bodies, I am afraid." Molly impatiently held up a towel. "Come on! Don't want to keep anyone waiting."

Willow stood up, snatched the towel, and wrapped it around

her quickly. "No need to get shy now, lass," fussed Molly as she picked up her dirty clothes and stopped to study each piece with curiosity. When she reached Willow's bra, she held it up by the strap, unsure of what to make of it.

Willow rushed over to where the robe hung and reached for it.

"Ye don't need to feign modesty on my account," said Molly. "I have seen more of yer kind come through here than I care to know about."

"What's that supposed to mean?" muttered Willow as she took the robe down and wrapped it around her.

"Never ye mind!" said Molly as she pulled out a small stool, motioned for Willow to sit, and roughly brushed her hair. When she was satisfied, she took Willow by the arm and pulled her into another bedroom. She pointed at the bed. "Wait in here. It won't be long!" She turned on her heels and left. Willow took a good look around the rather large room. This one was very cozy and comfortable indeed, with velvet red drapes on the windows and bed, and lit candles all around, giving off a soft warm glow. It had a few built-in shelves with books on them and a fireplace large enough to stand in, along with two leather chairs in front, one on each side. In the corner near the books stood a table holding several decanters of alcohol.

"This must be part of the premium package. I wonder who was lucky enough to get this room?" she asked aloud as she ran her fingers along the books on the shelf.

"That would be the Laird of the castle," a voice answered from the doorway.

Willow turned, relieved to finally see him. "Colin!" she exclaimed and met him halfway across the floor. "I have been calling out for you since I woke up. Where have you been and what on Earth happened last night? Everything is a little fuzzy."

Colin cocked his head at her oddly. "Have we met?"

"Ha-ha, very funny!" she said and jumped onto the bed. "Do you know what happened to my room? When I woke up this morning, everything was different. It is all very strange."

He folded his arms and stepped closer to her. "What makes you think I would know?"

She stretched out and used her hand to prop up her head. "Duh? You know everything that goes on around here. Isn't that what you do?"

He smirked. "That is indeed what I do, and I thought I knew of all happenings beneath this roof, but it seems I may have missed a few things."

She bit her lip as the previous evening came back into her mind. "What happened to us last night? The last thing I felt was your kiss on my lips and then everything went dark. I woke up this morning in a completely different room with no recollection of anything more."

He stroked his chin and attempted to conceal his amusement

as he stepped just to her side. "My kisses have been known to do that sort of thing to women."

Willow rolled her eyes. "If you say so, Romeo."

"I know so!" he purred, leaned over, and pressed his lips to hers, chastely at first before letting his tongue lazily explore her mouth. Her body reacted immediately; she let out a low moan as her hands instinctively went to his face. When she realized she touched hard flesh and not empty air, her eyes flew open wide, and she backed against the headboard, pulling her knees up in front of her as a barrier. "You're alive!" she shouted in disbelief.

"In more ways than one," he said and smirked down at the bulge rising from the fabric of his kilt. He climbed onto the bed toward her. "Tell me your name, lovely lass."

"You don't remember me?" she asked with a wounded and confused expression on her face.

"Oh, if we had met, I would remember you," he said as he pushed the part of her robe covering her knees open, exposing them.

"How is it you are alive?" she demanded, completely baffled and flustered.

He took his time and teased the top of one knee with the tip of his tongue before moving to the other, his hungry eyes locked on hers the whole while.

"I suppose it is because my time has not yet come," he replied before he suddenly slid his hands beneath her bottom, grasped her firmly, and jerked her down so they were face to face. "It's a good thing too because I would hate to leave this world without ever having had a taste of you."

He dropped his head and engulfed her mouth in one fluid motion.

Willow whimpered as he deftly untied her robe and laid it open while distracting her with his all-powerful kiss.

Dropping his head, he let out a delightful sigh as he took one nipple in his mouth, teasing and tasting it, while he used his fingers to tease and knead the other.

Willow's mind could think of nothing but his touch as she arched her back and pulled his head tighter to her breast, more than ready to lose herself in him completely. He raised his head and kissed her again. "Where has the whorehouse been hiding your sweetness?" he asked.

Willow froze, glared at him angrily, and pushed him away. "The what? You think I am a paid whore?"

He laughed softly. "I don't judge, after all, someone has to supply all these wonderful women to satisfy my urges before I am forced to take a wife, although I must say, I wish I had found you much sooner."

She shoved him off and pulled her robe back around to cover herself. "I can't believe you think I am a prostitute!" she said and smacked at him as she rolled off the bed.

"Forgive me, I did not mean to offend your so-called 'honor', but this is your occupation, is it not?"

"NO!" she shrieked. "It is NOT! I am not one of THOSE girls. I would never accept money for sex!"

His face grew dark. "Then what the hell are you doing in my bedchamber?"

Willow pressed her palm to her forehead. "That woman, Molly, brought me to this room. She told me she was getting me some clothes and to wait here—" she trailed off and looked up. "Wait! Did you just say you were getting married?"

He interlocked his fingers behind his head and crossed his feet, now genuinely curious about the mystery standing before him. "My brother is away making the arrangements now, and I am taking advantage of this time to spend it with women who WANT to be in the company of the Laird."

Willow started to back up, continuing until she felt her body hit the barrier of the stone wall. The blood drained from her face as she slid down it, feeling extremely sick to her stomach. Her eyes darted back and forth as things started to come together in her mind. "Molly is the woman who took care of you after your mother passed. Your brother, Brody, is away arranging your marriage to Sabina, a woman who despises you and you don't want to marry, but you must, or there will be a war with the MacDonnells," she mumbled to herself, her eyes darting side to side.

He suddenly rolled off the bed and firmly planted himself in front of her, his eyes narrowed. "How do you know all of this? Who are you?"

Wagging her finger, her attention turned to him. "Answer me one question. What year is it?"

Sighing, he shook his head and moved to the table to pour a glass of whiskey. "Leave it to Molly to bring me the one woman in this village whose mind is unwell."

"Please just answer the question," she whispered. "It is extremely important."

Exasperated, he turned and lifted his glass in the air. With a dramatic wave of his free hand, he crossly announced, "Milady, it is the year of our Lord, 1585."

His words slammed into her like a ton of bricks. She didn't know how or why, but somehow, she knew the words he spoke were true. "I was afraid of that," she whispered before slumping to one side and proceeding to black out.

"Bloody fecking hell!" Colin exclaimed as he slammed his glass down on the table and went over to check on her. After poking her arm a few times and realizing she was out cold, he gathered her up, carried her to the bed, and laid her across it. "Where, in God's name, did they find you?"

He grabbed a pillow and unceremoniously stuffed it under her head, but as he did, he noticed how utterly delicious she was. His gaze lingered. Reaching out to lightly touch her face with the back of his hand, he allowed his fingers to trace along the curve of her cheek. God, she was beautiful, probably the most desirable thing he had ever seen in his entire life, and he wanted badly to take her right then and there. Drawing his hand back, he reminded himself of the fact that unfortunately, she was most likely insane—and had a delicate constitution to boot.

His gaze drifted downward to see her robe had fallen open once more. He wrestled with his conscience as he stopped to enjoy the view of her perfectly shaped breasts, the ones he desperately wanted to taste again, and the more inviting sight of her neatly trimmed auburn mound. He reached out to touch her, cursed to himself, and instead, pulled her robe closed to cover her nakedness. What he had seen and tasted of her was delectable and he wanted far more, but he would never take a woman who was unwilling—or unconscious for that matter. He was no rapist, although she did seem extremely willing just a few moments earlier.

Taking a blanket from the foot of the bed, he pulled it across her. As he did, her eyes began to flutter open. After adjusting himself to conceal his desire, he went to the side table, picked up his glass, and brought it over to her.

When Willow came to, she was on the bed, covered with a blanket. Colin held a glass in front of her face.

"DRINK IT!" he ordered gruffly and helped her to sit up.

She eyed him warily but obeyed. The strong amber liquid splashed against the back of her throat, burning and causing her to cough and sputter.

Full of exasperation, he roughly patted her on the back until she was able to speak again.

"Thank you," she said softly.

He placed the glass on the table next to the bed. "Who are you and what the bloody hell are you doing here?"

"You wouldn't believe me if I told you," she muttered, pushing the hair back from her face.

"I think if you don't want to end up at the bottom of the loch, you had better start explaining! Start with your name!"

She blew out a deep breath and tried to figure out how best to handle the situation. "My name is Willow Mason. And for the record, I haven't the faintest idea how I ended up here."

"You said we knew each other and, I get the impression, very well, but I have never seen you before in my life," he pressed.

Well, he was half right. He had just never seen her in THIS life.

"I guess I was mistaken. It must have been someone else," she said, quietly, trying to brush off the question.

"Are you insinuating another is calling himself Colin MacLeod and taking liberties with women?" he demanded, visibly disturbed by the possibility.

"No—I mean, yes—I mean—but not the way you think—

it's all extremely complicated and I feel a sudden headache coming on," she stuttered.

"How do you know about the marriage and the details?"

"I must have overheard someone talking about it," she lied.

He watched her for a moment before going to the door. "MOLLY!" he bellowed, his eyes locked on Willow as he waited for the older woman to appear.

They had a brief, muffled conversation Willow could not hear, but it involved many hand gestures in her direction. He opened the door and urged the older woman into the hall. Molly waved him off and grumbled over her shoulder as she shuffled out. Colin bawled up his fists in frustration.

When he returned, he stood off to the side, frowning as he composed himself. "Molly is going to get you something more appropriate to wear and put you into a bedchamber. For the time being, you will be my guest until I figure out what is to be done with you, but, rest assured, if I find out you are here to do me or my family harm, I will not hesitate to kill you. Remember that! You will remain confined to your room especially given it is obvious you are not feeling well."

She nodded nervously. "Thank you. I will do as you ask."

"It was not a request!" he stated gruffly and departed.

6

CHAPTER SIX

Willow dropped her head into her hands. "What the actual fuck is going on here? How did this happen, and what the hell am I going to do?"

Molly came into the room shortly after Colin left. "Come on!" she ordered and escorted her back to the room she woke up in. "The Laird said to put ye in here so he could keep an eye on ye until the wedding."

"When exactly is the happy occasion?" she asked.

"When the bride and her family arrive in about two weeks. His brother, Brody, has made all the arrangements and will be back in a day or so with the final details."

She pulled a gown and a few other pieces from a chest in the corner, holding them up for comparison. "This should fit ye. Ye are about the same size Lady MacLeod was."

"Colin's mother, Mary?" she asked as she accepted the pile of clothing.

"He spoke of her to you?" Molly seemed surprised.

Willow winced. "He only mentioned her name, but it is clear he misses her."

Molly rested a hand on her hip and sighed nostalgically. "Aye, God rest her soul. She was a good one and that woman loved her babies more than anything." Molly turned to go. "I will be back to check on ye later."

When she heard the door close, Willow threw herself on the bed and wracked her brain for an explanation. "Finn's words!" she said aloud and snapped her fingers. "What was it about a kiss with no mortal lips and stating my desire?" She thought back over the previous night's activities. She had called out to the King of Fae, just before Colin kissed her.

"Fuck! I am actually in 1585, and I am so completely boned!"

After an hour of lying there in shock, she stood and dressed as best she could with everything she was given. Since she had no idea how most of the pieces were used, she simply slipped the gown on by itself and admired herself in a small hand mirror from a nearby dressing table. "Not bad!" she noted. She went to the door, quietly pulled it open, and looked down the hall. She was just about to sneak out when the door to the Laird's room flew open against the weight of an amorous couple who were stumbling out laughing.

Colin bid farewell to a beautiful woman who was giggling as she adjusted her skirts. The lady shoved some coins down the front of her gown, winked at him, and went in the other direction. He was rested against the doorframe with his arms folded and his feet crossed when he noticed Willow scowling at him angrily.

"Is something wrong?" he asked, vexed.

"Did you just have relations with that woman?"

He traipsed down the hall to her. "Aye, twice as a matter of fact," he smirked. "You weren't in any condition, and I needed some 'relief'. You see, Calyn is a seasoned professional, and I don't have to worry about her being of unsound mind or collapsing to the floor on me...well, without a good reason anyway," he taunted. "I have been known to make women weak with desire."

Willow raised her fingers to massage her temples. "So, you replaced me? Just like that?"

"Yes!" He nodded, smugly. "Why wouldn't I?"

"I can't believe you took another woman to bed! I knew you were a pervert who liked to watch women undress and do other things, but I didn't take you for someone who slept with just anyone. You are NOT the man I know!" she complained.

His face became enraged. "No, I am not the man you know because I DON'T KNOW YOU! Woman, we have never met!" he shouted, completely bothered. "And I am not a pervert!" He looked her up and down. "Why are you out of your room anyway? I ordered you to stay inside."

She looked down. "Half of me is inside, technically, and now, so is the rest!" she retorted and slammed the door in his face.

An infuriated Colin glared at the door, which had just been shut by a woman who claimed to know him. It was time to get to the bottom of this, once and for all, because the sooner he did, the sooner he would be rid of her. She was an unwelcome distraction, so much so in fact, he had not even bedded Calyn when she came to his room. He had been too preoccupied to pay her any mind even though she had done her best to pique his interests. Finally, after an hour, he had just paid her extra to leave and sent her on her way.

He shoved the door open and stormed inside. She stood at the window and did not bother to acknowledge him when he came in.

"Who are you?" he demanded. "And why do you care so much about who I bed anyway? Are you a MacDonnell sent here to spy on me?"

"Fuck who you wish! It's none of my business," she replied as she tried to appear disinterested and glided across the floor to sit down at the small dressing table. Picking up a rudimentary brush, she pulled it through her wavy locks, frowning when it tangled and tugged.

He moved behind her and lightly touched her hair. "What if I decide to make it my business to feck you?"

She slammed the brush down. "You won't!" she said nonchalantly.

"You seem very sure of yourself," he said as he caught a strand of her hair in his hand and leaned down to smell the fresh, clean lavender scent coming off her skin.

"I am!"

Suddenly, he roughly grabbed her around the waist, dragged her to the bed, and threw her across it. Climbing atop her, he pinned her arms above her head with one hand and moved his face close to hers. "Tell me! Are you still so certain I won't ravage you here and now?"

She looked him directly in the eye, confident on the outside, a little less so on the inside. "Colin MacLeod refuses to take a woman against her will and, since I have not consented, I know you will not dare."

"You seemed willing enough an hour ago," he countered as he felt his desire immediately spring to life. Pressing it against her upper thigh, he brushed his nose against her neck. "Why should I think you have changed your mind?"

She raised her head. "I WAS willing an hour ago until you accused me of being a whore and now, I am not, so kindly get off me unless you intend to rape me here and now."

He hesitated, cursed silently to himself, and rolled off her.

He stood, went to the door, and glanced back. "You will remain in this room!" he commanded. Once he was in the hall, he locked the door and gripped the key tightly in his hand. He didn't know who she was or what she wanted, but at least he would know where she was at all times.

Willow sat straight up on the bed when she heard the jingle of a key. "No! No! NO!" She rushed to the door and tried to open it, but it was no use because he had locked it.

Damn it! She pushed him too far and this was the price. She pressed her back against the door and tried to pull her thoughts together. Somehow, someway, she had ended up stuck in 1585, with a man who didn't recognize her, because, in fact, they had not met, she had no idea how or why she was here, and she was utterly alone. She could only assume she was here to save Colin from becoming a ghost by stopping the MacLeod family from being slaughtered, but that might prove difficult at best if she couldn't even get out of this room.

The wedding would be the key. If she could stop it, Sabina and Brody would never be caught in bed together and the slaughter would never happen. Maybe if she could get him to call it off and change his fate, perhaps she would be sent back home as easily and quickly as she was brought here.

The sun was sinking low in the sky when the door rattled and finally opened.

Willow leaped to her feet and watched as Molly brought in a tray with a plate of food and a bottle of whiskey. "I can't have ye starving to death up here," she said as she placed it on the nearby table and turned to look at her.

"He locked me in," said Willow, her growling stomach urging her over to the table. Her supper consisted of some sort of stew and a chunk of bread. Molly poured some of the whiskey into a glass and placed it in front of her. "Aye, and he intends to keep ye here until he gets what he wants."

"What exactly DOES he want?" asked Willow warily, breaking off a piece of bread and stuffing it into her mouth.

"I expect there are TWO things he wants if I know him, but he wants to know who ye are first of all."

Willow groaned. "I have already told him my name."

"That's not what I mean." Molly put one hand on her hip. "Who are ye, and what are ye doing here, lass?"

Willow pulled up a chair and sat down. "I honestly don't know. I have no idea how I even got here," she replied—and it was the truth.

"Ye don't remember how ye got here?" Molly watched her closely. "Did ye hit yer head or something? Ye did faint after all."

An idea came into Willow's mind, and she slowly nodded. "You know what, Molly, I believe I did." She sighed as she rubbed an imaginary spot on her head and slumped her shoulders dramatically. "I have had a horrible headache all day and there are some things I just can't, for the life of me, recall."

"Well, there ye go!" Molly patted her on the back comfortingly. "Ye have had an accident and that explains it. Ye just need some rest, and ye will be as right as rain!" She handed her the glass. "Eat yer supper and drink this. Ye'll feel better in the morning."

She shuffled over to the door and said, "I will see ye when I bring yer breakfast."

"Molly!" she called out. "What's the other thing he wants?"

"What does every man want?" Molly stopped, turned, and pointed at her. "The Laird has been whoring his way through every willing and available woman in the village for as long as I can remember, but more so the past week. Ye are the one woman who has not found yer way into his bed. Yer a smart girl, and I'm sure ye can figure it out," and she left.

Willow dropped her bread on the plate in disgust. "Whoring his way through the village for as long as she can remember? Seriously? I knew he was too good to be true."

"Well?" he asked impatiently when Molly came out of the room. He had been trying to listen to their conversation with his ear pressed to the door, but he couldn't hear anything. "What did she say? What did you find out? Did she ask about me?"

Molly tugged on his arm until he leaned down so she could whisper in his ear. Instead, she plucked him between the eyes. "What are ye? An unwed maid trying to find out from the other lasses what the stable boy said about yer tits and yer arse?"

Colin frowned and gave her a dirty look. "Just tell me!"

"Hmph!" she cut her eyes at him. "The poor girl hit her head, and she is confused to the point she can't think straight, that's what! What's the matter with ye? Not enough willing and able women left in the village for ye to wet yer prick with? Ye have got to start taking the injured and sick ones too?"

An affronted Colin raised his voice, "YOU are the one who put her in my room! If this is anyone's fault, it is yours."

Molly started down the hall. "That's right! Let's blame the old woman because the one lass ye wish to lure into yer bed won't let ye anywhere near her honeypot! Put it all on me if it makes ye feel better and gets ye through the night. It's not like ye can blame her! Ye do have her locked up like a prisoner."

Colin made a face behind her back as she went.

"I saw that, ye wee shite! See if I wash yer bed sheets tomorrow after ye get done pleasuring yerself on them tonight while ye are having lustful dreams about that pretty lass!" she yelled over her shoulder.

He chuckled to himself, amused by her words. Molly had a heart of gold, but she covered it up with snarky comments, hard truths, and filthy language. He relocked the door, went back to his room, and over to the table holding the decanters of alcohol. As he tried to figure out what the woman was up to, he swallowed a glassful of whiskey, and his eyes went to his bookcase. An idea suddenly occurred to him. Maybe he COULD get more flies with honey.

Willow finished her meal and sat in front of the fireplace, nursing the rather strong whiskey she was slowly becoming accustomed to while trying to figure out how to get out of the damn room she was locked up in. A light knock at the door, and the sound of the key turning, made her look up. She was surprised to see Colin standing there with three books in hand. She waited for him to speak.

"I noticed you looking at my book collection earlier, and I thought you might want something to read. You can read, can't you?"

"Very well actually," she replied. "Thank you. It was kind of you to think of me."

He placed them on the bed and walked over to the fireplace. Taking a splinter of wood from the pile, he lit it and used it to light the candles on the mantle. He tossed it into the burning pile when he was done and turned to face her. "Molly said you had an accident, and you were having trouble remembering things."

"So, it would seem," she lied.

"You should have told me before, because it explains a great deal." He picked up the bottle from the tray and refilled her glass. "I think we may have gotten off on the wrong foot, and I would like to rectify that."

"For future reference, assuming a woman you just met is from the whorehouse sent to sleep with you is not the best way to introduce yourself," she snapped.

"The lady may have a point," he conceded with a nod as he located another glass and poured himself a drink. "I will strive to remember that in the future." He took the seat next to her. "Why did you think I was dead when we first met?"

She looked down into her glass. "I was just confused, that's all."

"You were not confused about the information on my upcoming nuptials, and you did not hear about it from anyone inside this castle. No one has seen you here before this morning, and this union has not been formally announced. I need to know where you got it from."

"You wouldn't believe me if I told you," she whispered, her eyes still cast downward.

He reached out suddenly and grabbed her arm tightly.

"OW! You are hurting me!" she exclaimed.

He loosened his grip only slightly. "I am afraid I must insist. You see, there is a great deal at stake, and if you are a MacDonnell sent here to gather information or to lay in some sort of plan to do harm, I cannot allow that to happen. I am trying to maintain peace between the families, and I will not allow anyone to jeopardize what I am building."

"I am not here to hurt anyone!" she said and yanked her arm free.

"Why won't you tell me then?" he demanded.

"Because you will think I am mad, or worse, and I prefer not to end up being burned at the stake."

"Are you a witch?" he asked.

"No!"

"Then you have nothing to fear!"

She simply shook her head and remained silent.

He stood. "Very well. You will remain locked in this room until you have something more to tell me." And he left.

Willow went over to the bed, laid down, curled into a ball, and burst into tears. Lost and alone, she had no idea what to do next. She sobbed herself to sleep and woke up sometime in the middle of the night with a slight pain on the bottom of her foot. Ignoring it, she rolled over and went back to sleep.

7

CHAPTER SEVEN

Willow spent the following day alone searching every nook and cranny of the room for a way out and, while she did locate the peepholes to the secret room, they were no help to her whatsoever. She even considered climbing out of the window, but it was a little high up and there weren't any modern hospitals nearby if she fell. The only person she saw or spoke to was Molly when she brought her meals, and she did not linger with the Laird impatiently waiting in the hall.

By late evening, she had started to feel tired and a little unwell, so she turned in early. At some point in the night, she was awakened by a terrible stabbing pain. She tossed back the covers and saw her foot was red, swollen, and inflamed. Sweat dripped from her brow and she realized she was running a high fever. Limping over to the window, she tried to throw it open to let in some cool air to blow against her face but ended up falling to the floor instead. As she faded in and out of consciousness, a smiling woman dressed in white appeared in front of her, kneeled, and reached out to touch her face.

"Don't worry, Willow," she said. "My name is Mary, and I will watch over you."

"Mary?" she whispered, now panting and completely drenched in perspiration. She watched the woman throw open the window just before her sight dimmed and everything went black. She must have been found on the floor in the same spot the following morning because the next thing she remembered was the feeling of being picked up and laid across the bed. Then came the sensation of someone placing a cold rag to her forehead and forcing some water to her lips before she slipped into oblivion again.

Colin unlocked the door while Molly waited with a tray of food. He did not trust anyone else with the key to the room holding this woman, not even her. He wanted to make sure she did not get away from him before he knew more about her.

"How long are ye going to keep her in there?" asked Molly. "Are ye so afraid of that scrawny little lass ye need to keep her hidden away, or are ye just trying to keep her all to yerself?

"What's that supposed to mean?"

Molly grinned, exposing a few missing teeth. "I have seen the way ye look at her. She is getting under yer skin, and I don't think it's just because she won't let ye into her bed. I think ye might be feeling something more for her."

He huffed. "She has been here less than three days, and it's not nearly enough time for her to get 'under my skin'!"

"Yer father fell in love with yer mother when he first laid eyes on her. Sometimes, it is less about time and more about how a person makes ye feel."

"You want to know how she makes me feel?" He tightened his jaw. "She annoys the shite out of me!"

Molly laughed. "That's exactly what yer mother said one day after she met yer father. I suppose the apple doesn't fall far from the tree!" She went around him and into the room, leaving him to sulk.

He rushed in when he heard the tray clamber to the floor, and Molly call out for help. The first thing he saw when he stepped inside was Willow in a heap by the window, and Molly with her hand pressed to her face trying to wake her.

"She is burning with fever! Get her into bed!"

Colin gathered her up and laid her down, careful not to jostle her too much. "Call for the healer, Molly!" he commanded before going to the nearby wash basin, wringing out a cloth and placing it across her forehead. When she began to cough and wheeze, he loosened the ties on her dress and wiped the sweat from her neck and chest.

"Damn it!" he whispered. "This is all my fault for keeping

you locked in this stuffy room without any fresh air. I should have known better."

"Colin," she called out and her eyes flew open wide, but she was delirious and out of her mind.

He took her by the hand and brushed the hair back from her face. "I am here."

"I won't let your family die," she muttered to no one, her eyes now closed and her head rolling from side to side. "I'll stop it! I swear! I care for you too much to let your soul be stuck in this house for all eternity."

He looked at her oddly. "You care for me?" he asked, bewildered.

She tried to raise up, but he gently pushed her back down. Her eyes opened again and locked in on his. "You didn't deserve it. You didn't kill them, and you shouldn't be a ghost stuck here for four hundred years. Where is the King of the Fae? I have to find him!"

She frowned, then laughed. "God help me, I'm in love with a ghost."

His blood ran cold as he watched her intently. "A ghost? I am a ghost?"

"Not if I can help it," she said and burst into tears.

He stared at her blankly until his father shouted his name, breaking his concentration.

Molly yelled down to the main hall from the balcony overlooking it. "Find Samuel, the healer!" she barked, and three younger girls scattered in different directions.

"Who is ill?" called up Stewart MacLeod, concerned. "Is it Colin?"

"Nay! It is the woman the Laird has kept locked in the back bedchamber for the past few days," she replied and ordered another woman who passed by to bring up a fresh pitcher of water.

"Locked up? What woman?" asked Stewart confused. "Is she one of his whores?"

"Nay!" Molly shook her head. "This was the only one who has had enough sense to turn him away from her bed!"

Molly turned to go back into the room leaving Stewart to wonder what was going on as he ascended the stairs.

"Colin! Colin!" Who the devil is this woman and why are ye holding her in this room?" demanded Stewart as he came across the threshold.

"Keep your voice down!" He slowly lifted his head to look at his father. "Her name is Willow, and she showed up here a couple of days ago. I thought she might be a MacDonnell here to cause trouble, but now, I don't think she is."

"Why have ye not mentioned her?" He came over to get a

better look at the sickly woman.

Colin shook his head. "I don't know. I just haven't."

"What's wrong with her?" asked his father.

Colin closed his eyes and gripped her hand tighter. "She is sick with fever, and it is my fault for keeping her up here."

A tall, thin older man with a long beard hurried into the room, and Colin quickly moved so the man could examine her. He looked her over, pulling at her clothes, and searching her entire body until he located the source of the illness. "Her foot is infected," he said as he touched it, causing her to rise and cry out in pain.

Colin moved back to her side and put his arm around her. He gently rocked and shushed her to calm her as Samuel poked and prodded at the wound. Tapping the side of his temple, the healer thought for a moment before giving instructions to a young boy who accompanied him and sending him off. "I will make a poultice to draw the infection off. It's the best course of action right now." Samuel moved around the bed to the other side, felt her forehead, and frowned.

"Let them tend her," said Stewart and took his son by the arm. "We need to speak alone."

Colin reluctantly laid her back down and followed his father into the hall.

"Why are ye keeping this woman locked up and a secret?" Stewart demanded.

"It was just to find out what her game was," he replied and looked back at the door.

"And?"

Colin clenched his fists. "I just don't know!"

Stewart gripped his forearm and said in a low voice. "Ye have a wife who will be here in less than two weeks, and this woman needs to be gone by then. If ye only want to feck her, do it and be done with it, but, if there's more to it, then find her a discreet place in the village where ye can stow her away from watchful eyes. We cannot allow anything, or anyone, to disrupt this very uneasy alliance we have made with the MacDonnells. Ye have a duty as Laird to maintain this peace between the families."

"I am very aware of my 'duties', Father! I don't need you to remind me."

Stewart leaned closer. "Then act like it. I do not have much time left in this world, and I will see this family safe before I join yer mother in the next. Get all of this out of yer system before the MacDonnells arrive."

Colin gritted his teeth in disgust and watched his father walk away. He took a deep breath, went back into the room, and watched closely as Samuel made a mixture of some sort with the items brought back by the boy, smeared it on her foot, and wrapped it up.

"The poultice should help pull out the infection," he said

when he was finished. "It's important to get water into her as well, especially with her fever being so high."

"I will see it gets done," said Colin and pulled a blanket over her.

The healer gathered his things. "Send for me if anything changes, otherwise, I will check back in a bit."

"I will stay with her," offered Molly as she changed out the basin water.

"No, I will do it," Colin said and pulled a chair over to the bed.

Molly moved the refilled bowl to the table closest to them, turned around, and gently placed her hand on his shoulder.

"She is not yer mother, boy, and there is no reason to think she will meet the same fate. I have a feeling this one has a good deal of fight in her."

He covered her hand with his own. "I hope you're right, Molly."

After Molly left, he placed a fresh cloth on her head and looked over at the cup on the table. He gathered her up, pulled her against him, and tried to make her drink, but she spat it all back out. He tried twice more to no avail. "Well, this isn't working," he said and gently laid her back down.

A thought occurred to him. He took a sip of the water, leaned over, and lightly pressed his lips to hers. She greedily lifted her chin and her lips slightly parted, an invitation for more. As he dribbled the water into her mouth, she readily accepted his gift. He repeated the action until he had emptied an entire cup, and she seemed to settle comfortably.

"Is there any change?" asked Molly when she brought in supper for him later that evening.

"No! Her fever still rages, but at least she sleeps and is not as restless as she was," he replied as he looked over at Willow.

"Ye need to get some rest yerself," she said as she handed him a plate.

"I will rest here," he replied, accepting the dish and setting it aside. Leaning back in his chair, he rubbed his eyes. "Has Brody returned from the MacDonnell lands yet?"

"Aye!" Molly nodded. "Just a little while ago. He is waiting to speak with ye."

"I suppose that means all the arrangements have been made," he muttered with the enthusiasm of a man planning his own funeral.

Molly sat down in the chair next to him and folded her hands in her lap. "Colin, ye don't have to do this, ye know. Yer a grown man, and ye are entitled to make yer own decisions without having to honor the ones yer father pushes ye into. Yer poor mother would be rolling in her grave if she thought for one moment a bairn of hers was getting married for anything less than love."

"My mother did not have to worry about keeping so many people out of harm's way. We have been on the verge of war with the MacDonnells for years, but not nearly as close as we have been the past few months. A battle with them will serve no one, only take lives unnecessarily on both sides, and I will not allow that to happen to you or anyone else under my protection. We will have peace here, no matter what the cost, and if the price is being in a loveless marriage, then I will gladly pay it."

"Surely, there is another way," she fussed. "Marrying a lass ye have never met and, care nothing for, is not the answer."

He blew out a long breath. "Then tell me what is? This marriage and a shared child will be the only thing needed to unite these two families for the future. One family dare not attack the other once that occurs and, as Laird, I must lead by example."

"And what of this child who grows up in a home where his mother and father care naught for each other? What kind of life is that for yer son or yer daughter?"

He wiped his brow. "A safe one—and who's to say we won't grow to love each other in time? Even if we don't, this will at the very least, give Brody and my future children the gift of choosing who they wish to love."

Molly looked over at Willow. "Ye can't give yer heart to another when it is already taken and, boy, yers already is."

"I don't know what you mean, Molly."

She reached over and took his hand. "Aye, ye do. Ye fell for that lass over there when ye first laid eyes on her. She is something special, and yer heart knows it even if yer head doesn't. Ye will never be satisfied with another, and ye are only asking for misery if ye marry the MacDonnell woman."

He squeezed her hand. "I am old enough for my wants not to hurt me, and besides, I gave all of them up when I became Laird."

Molly wrinkled her nose at him. "Well, I'm not giving up hope ye will come to yer senses and end up with the right woman in yer bed for a change." She stood and kissed him on the forehead. "I promised yer mother on her deathbed I would look after the lot of ye, and I mean to do it." Molly started out of the room and called over her shoulder, "Eat yer supper and get some sleep ye wee shite, and don't be taking advantage of that poor girl by accosting her while she is asleep." She stopped at the door and grinned back at him.

"Aye, milady." He chuckled softly. "I will do my best."

He ate his supper and settled in for the night in a chair pulled up to the bed. The following morning, there was no change in her condition, and he was visibly upset by the time the healer arrived.

"Can't you do anything else?" he shouted at Samuel.

"I am doing all I can do, my Laird," he replied gently. "Give the poultice time to work." Samuel placed his hand on his shoulder. "Just keep doing what ye are doing and pray. It is all we can do."

Colin nodded and watched him leave as Brody came into the room.

"Here you are. Molly said you were holding up in here, tending to someone who was sick with a fever." Brody caught sight of Willow and stopped short. "Now, I see why! Who is this beauty?"

Colin shook his head, took his brother by the arm, and pulled him away from the bed toward the fireplace. "Her name is Willow Mason."

"Where in the world did you find her?" asked Brody.

"She found me. I thought she was sent here to sabotage the truce, but I am fairly certain now I was mistaken."

"What makes you so sure?"

"Some of the things she has said in her delirium have convinced me otherwise and besides, I just have a feeling." Colin leaned against the wall.

Brody raised his eyebrows. "Are you sure your 'feelings' aren't being clouded by something else—like your cock? They do tend to muddy things up a bit, especially for MacLeod men."

"I have not lain with her if that is what you are insinuating!" Colin said and rolled his eyes.

Brody stepped toward the bed. "Why not? Did she turn you down?"

Colin growled at him causing Brody to hold up his hands in

a defensive posture, smirking. "A sore spot, I see," he goaded.

"What news do you bring from the MacDonnells?" asked Colin to change the subject.

Brody sighed and his smile faded. "The bargain is struck. They will arrive in a few days and the two of you will be wed, although I can't for the life of me understand why Father is so insistent upon this happening so quickly."

Colin wiped his face with his hand. "He has his reasons."

"What reasons?" demanded Brody. "Does it have anything to do with him making you Laird?"

"Never mind! This is for the best. I just want to get it over with so I can be done with it."

Brody placed his hand on Colin's shoulder. "Are you sure about this?"

"I have no other choice, brother. You know that."

Brody looked over at Willow. "I also know some things may have changed in my absence. You had a different woman in your bed each night before I left, and now, you are keeping vigil over one woman you have never lay with. Perhaps your feelings on the matter are different now?"

Colin patted his brother on the back. "My feelings are of no matter because my obligations are the same, and I intend to honor them."

Brody dropped his head. "Then I will take care of the preparations while you are tending to other issues." He turned and left the room.

Colin went back to her side when he noticed her arm had fallen from beneath the covers. He carefully took her hand, kissed it, and pressed his cheek to the back of it. Her head shifted a bit toward him, and he reached to smooth back her hair. "What are you doing here, Willow Mason?"

Colin remained by her side the whole day and half the night until her fever finally broke. When he noticed it had abated, he closed his eyes and thanked God for His mercy. He sat down in the chair next to her and dozed off as his exhaustion caught up with him.

8

CHAPTER EIGHT

Willow's eyes slowly fluttered open as she started to come around. Everything on her hurt and when she tried to shift, her body stiffened, slow to respond. Her mouth was dry, and a cold ache had settled into her bones, causing her to shiver all over. Turning her head, she saw a cup on the side table. She reached for it but ended up knocking it over instead. "Shit!" she muttered and fell back against the pillow.

"Let me get that for you," she heard Colin say, apparently startled awake. He picked up the cup, refilled it, and sat down on the edge of the bed. Slipping his arm around her shoulders, he helped her to sit up and sip the water.

"Thank you," she said gratefully and looked around. "What happened?"

After gently resting her back upon the pillows, he set the cup aside, tucked the blanket around her legs, and wiped the sleep from his eyes with his palm. "It seems you injured your foot on something, and it became infected. You developed an extremely high fever. Molly found you collapsed on the floor by the window when she brought in your breakfast. The fever finally broke a few hours ago."

"How long have I been out?" she asked, wincing as she stretched out her leg, the pain from her foot shooting upward.

"Two days and two nights," he replied. She tried to get up, but he stopped her. "You are in no condition to leave this bed anytime soon."

Damn it. She had lost almost a week, and the wedding would be here soon.

"I'm fine!" she said and tried again but fell back.

"Obviously, you are not. You are as weak as a kitten and, even if you weren't, you do not need to be on that foot." He scratched his head. "Where are your shoes anyway? I have searched this whole damn room and found no trace of them."

Apparently, the King of the Fae didn't deem it necessary to send them along, she thought to herself.

"I don't know," she simply said.

He sighed. "I will find some for you immediately, and I will have Molly bring up some broth for you to help you regain your strength. If you need or want anything, just ask and, and, if it is in my power, I will provide it."

Willow eyed him cautiously. "Why are you being so nice to

me suddenly? Aren't you convinced I am here to do you harm?"

"I was, but I don't believe so anymore. We can discuss it later when you are feeling better," he half-smiled. "I am merely glad to see you are recovering. Others have not been as fortunate when the fever overtakes them." He glanced sadly toward the chest.

"Your mother passed of fever?" she asked.

He nodded. "It took her quickly and changed my life forever. I am just pleased you did not meet the same fate." He rose. "REST!" he commanded and left the room.

Molly came in a little while later with a steaming bowl in hand. "Well, it's good to see ye awake! How are ye feeling, lass?"

Willow pushed up on her elbows and leaned back against the headboard. "I think it's too soon to tell."

Molly sat down on the edge of the bed and spooned out some of the broth. "Open up!" The older woman held out her hand with the spoon.

"I can manage, but thank you," she said and took the bowl.

"Ye had us all right worried," pointed out Molly. "I haven't seen the Laird this upset since his mother died. He insisted on being by yer side the whole time."

Willow blew on a spoonful of broth and raised it to her lips. "Colin? I got the distinct impression he would have just as soon seen me die. It would have been much more convenient for him, I'm sure."

"Hardly!" Molly waved her hand. "Don't let him fool ye! The Laird has developed a soft spot for ye, and a special sort of itch if I am not mistaken—one only ye can scratch."

"He probably picked up a rash from those hundreds of women he has been fucking," she muttered under her breath.

Molly raised her eyebrows, then burst into laughter. "I like ye, lass," she said and patted her leg. "I think ye are just what that wee shite needs. If ye need anything at all, just call out. I will leave the door open a bit."

"I thought I was on lockdown?" questioned a surprised Willow.

"Not anymore. The Laird says ye can come and go as ye wish—as long as ye are feeling up to it, that is."

Three days later, Willow was feeling much better thanks to a great deal of Colin's forced rest by his constant checking in and Molly's cooking. He kept her entertained by reading to her each afternoon, and she was touched he took so much time from his busy day to be with her. Their interactions had become warmer and more light-hearted with each passing day, and Willow felt herself rapidly falling in love with him. Her foot was well on the way to being healed, and she was able to hobble about a bit.

She overheard some of the servants say the MacDonnells

would be there in three days, and she still had no idea how to stop this wedding. Realizing she needed to do something, she asked Molly to bring up a basin of water to wash with and some clean clothes so she could get moving. Willow slowly cleaned herself and, once she was presentable, she limped down to Colin's room and tapped on the door.

"Come in!" he called out.

She pushed open the door and hopped in, leaning against the wall for support.

"What are you doing up?" he fussed and got up from his small desk. "You should still be in bed." He stomped over, swept her off her feet, and carried her to a chair.

"I was hoping for some fresh air?" she asked, cautiously. "I have been stopped up in that room for too long, and I am going a little stir crazy."

He crossed his arms and gave her a stern, disapproving look.

"Oh, come on! I will be good, and it's not like I can run away." She held out her still puffy foot. "Please? Pretty please?"

His face softened a bit. "Alright! But I will carry you to somewhere where you can sit down, and I will personally make sure you behave."

"Fair enough," she conceded.

He gathered her up in his arms, carried her downstairs and outside into the glorious sunshine.

Willow got her first good look at the castle, and she marveled at the beauty of it now, compared to what it would be in the future. The difference was night and day, and it made her smile. Once they were outside, he looked for somewhere to put her down. "How about the top of the hill where the rose bushes are?" she asked and pointed.

He glanced in the direction and frowned.

"Please?" she asked sweetly.

He let out a resigned sigh and proceeded. As he placed her on the stone bench, her eyes went to the headstone, now new, as opposed to the ancient one she had found by chance in the future.

He joined her.

"How long has she been gone?" asked Willow, sympathetically.

"Ten years." He broke off a single rosebud and handed it to her. "Roses were her favorite, and I wanted to make sure she was surrounded by them always."

Willow smiled and inhaled the sweet fragrance. "My mother's favorite was daisies. She has been gone for four years. It never seems to get any easier, does it?"

He shook his head. "No, it does not. I still miss her every single day."

"And I miss him," a voice said. The stunning figure she had seen when she was ill appeared behind him and rested her hand on his shoulder. "My sweet, handsome baby boy. He visits my grave each day, rain or shine, and will allow no one to tend the roses he planted around it, save him."

"Mary was it?" asked Willow. They nodded simultaneously and much in the same way. There was no mistaking they were mother and son.

Mary looked up. "Tell him what you can do. Tell him about your gift."

Willow winced. "I prefer not to be burned at the stake," she muttered.

A curious expression filled his face. "Why do you keep saying that?" he asked.

Mary tilted her head, encouragingly.

Willow closed her eyes and blew out a long breath as she twisted the stem between her fingers. "Because it is what they do to people in this time when someone says they can see and talk to the dead."

His head turned slowly, choosing his words carefully before he spoke. "You are not yet fully recovered from your fever. Your mind is still clouded."

Mary moved to stand in front of her marker and looked down at it. "Tell him I am here, and you can prove it."

Willow groaned and shook her head vigorously.

"Go on!" urged Mary. "What good is your gift if you don't use it?"

Tightening her lips, she hesitated. "Your mother is here," she finally acknowledged begrudgingly.

Colin rose to his feet and set his jaw. "You should be in bed, resting. I should never have agreed to let you come out so soon."

"Tell him his parents met when his father kidnapped his mother for ransom."

Willow blinked and did a double take of Mary. "His father kidnapped you?"

Colin's head snapped to attention.

Mary nodded as she turned around. "On my wedding day to another man, no less. He hatched a plan to bring more money in for the estate. He would kidnap the daughter of a wealthy and influential family in London and ask for a substantial ransom in return. I was in my wedding gown, preparing to go to the church, when he burst into the room, put a blade to my throat, and forced me outside where he placed me atop his horse and took us to the dock. He held me on a ship he sailed and anchored safely away from shore. When he went to pick up the ransom, two days later, he sent a note back to my father thanking him for the 'dowry' and informing him he had decided he had fallen hopelessly in love with me and planned to take me as his wife. The final line in his letter assured him he would take exceptionally good care of his daughter. I despised him for what he did, but he pulled anchor and set sail, and I had no say in the matter. Each night, he brought me supper and a gift, whether it be a jewel or a seashell, he always had something in hand. By the time we reached MacLeod lands, my heart had softened, I was utterly in love, and there was no going back. My father's men arrived three days later, just in time for our nuptials. I sent them back with a letter telling my father I was happily married and would remain with my husband until my dying day."

"What a romantic story," gushed Willow. "It sounds just like a fairytale."

"Tell him what I just told you," she pressed.

Willow related the story and watched the blood drain from Colin's face. "How could you possibly know that? Who told you? Molly?"

Willow shook her head. "I told you already—it was your mother!"

"You are lying!" His face filled with rage, and he fumed.

Mary tapped her finger to her lips as she thought of a better way to convince him. "Tell him I used to call him my little 'mockingbird'. When he was seven years old, he came running down to breakfast one morning with his eyes red, filled with tears and embraced me as tightly as he could. I asked him what was wrong, and he informed me, he was sure I had died in the night, and he was just so happy to see me still alive. When I asked why he believed such a thing, he said he had come to our bedroom door in the middle of the night and heard his father moaning as if in pain, and calling out the words, "Oh Mary! I will not rest until I have sent ye to Heaven this night!" He then heard the banging on the walls and me crying out the words, "Don't stop, my love! I am almost there! He then heard me scream out, in what he thought, was pain, even though it was quite the opposite."

Willow covered her mouth with her hand and snorted.

"The twenty guests we had at the breakfast table the following morning had the same reaction you just did," Mary chuckled, "Needless to say, from then on, we always made sure he was fast asleep before we made love."

Willow burst into laughter. "Mockingbird! I am guessing your guests were thoroughly entertained by that little tidbit of information."

"Indeed, they were!" she snickered behind her hand. "Stewart and I were never able to live that one down. I even heard mention of it at my funeral, for goodness sake. But, oh what a night it was, and one of my fondest memories!"

Colin's eyes went wild as he looked back and forth between Willow and the empty space she was speaking to.

"What sort of demon are you?" he demanded.

Willow rolled her eyes and turned her attention back to Mary. "What's keeping you here, Mary? Why haven't you moved on?"

Mary smiled. "I am simply waiting for my love, Stewart. He is unwell and will be joining me soon enough. We will cross over into the next world together when his time comes." Mary looked back at Colin. "I will be leaving my little 'mockingbird' in your very capable hands. I have no doubt you will straighten him out and get him to quit laying with half of the women in Scotland. Seriously, it's disgusting!"

Mary winked and slowly faded out.

"Your mother is adorable!" She turned to face Colin. "First of all, I am no demon. God bestowed a gift upon me at birth, and I have been able to bring many people a great deal of comfort with messages from their loved ones."

"My mother's soul is trapped here?" he asked, the thought appalling to him.

"No, she is simply waiting for your father. I am sorry to be the one to tell you this, but she says he is ill, and he won't be around much longer."

He made his way back over to her side and sat down. "He has sworn Samuel, the healer, to secrecy and told no one, save me, he is ill. It is why he went forward with making me Laird." He looked down at the grave and, in the moment, reminded Willow of a lost child looking for his parents. "Are you certain my mother is not suffering?"

"Not in the least!" She took his hand. "She seems happy to me, but she does miss you terribly."

His eyes welled. "Not nearly as much as I miss her." He brushed a tear from his cheek. "You have told me this much, now will you please tell me about the other things you have been keeping from me? Don't say there isn't more because I know there is."

"You won't believe me!"

He sighed. "Why don't you give me a chance to make up my own mind? I think I have earned it."

Willow squeezed his hand. "Alright! Here goes. If you marry Sabina, everyone in this castle, all your family and the people you care for, including yourself, will die."

"How could you possibly know something like that?" he asked aghast.

She hesitated for a long moment before she eyed him cautiously and answered, "Because, in the year 2016, your ghost told me everything."

Colin thought he had heard wrong at first, but the serious expression on her face told him differently. Was this woman honestly trying to tell him she came from the year 2016 and his own ghost warned her about his death? It was ridiculous, and this woman must truly be insane. No one could travel through time— or could they? Up until a few short moments ago, he didn't believe anyone could talk to the dead, either, yet she knew things only his mother would have been able to tell her. He had a feeling from the beginning there was something special about this woman and his instincts had never failed him before. He remained silent and listened intently as she explained her entire story to him and, when she was done, a chill ran down his spine and he sat as still as stone.

Great, she broke him.

Willow knew he wouldn't believe her, but she had expected him to rage and call her all sorts of names, become angry even— not become frozen in a catatonic state.

"It's not possible," he finally uttered.

"Up until fifteen minutes ago, you didn't think anyone could talk to the dead," she said dryly. "I will swear on a stack of Bibles, what I speak is the truth, and I can prove it. Just ask Brody if he has fallen in love with your future wife."

"He would never do that to me," he said.

"Yeah, because no one in your family falls in love at the drop of a hat," she retorted dryly.

He raked his hands through his hair. "Even if it is true, it is of no matter. She is pledged to the Laird of this estate and, if we do not marry, war will break out."

"It will if you do, as well!" She closed her eyes and suddenly felt tired and weak. She wobbled a bit; his face filled with concern.

"You should be in your room." He picked her up, carried her back upstairs, and tucked her in. "I will check on you later. Do not leave this bed!" he ordered.

She moaned slightly, turned on her side, and fell fast asleep. He rested his hand on her shoulder, and she let out a peaceful sigh. He leaned over and brushed a strand of hair from her face before leaving to find out if what she said was true.

9

CHAPTER NINE

"Why would you accuse me of such a thing?" demanded Brody of his brother as he paced the floor.

Colin leaned back in his chair and studied his little brother.

"You think I would betray you in such a way?"

"Just answer me truthfully. I will not be angry, I give you my word, but you must be completely upfront and honest with me. Many lives may depend on it."

Brody's breathing became labored, and his shoulders slumped as he stared down at the floor

Colin knew at that moment Willow had spoken the truth.

"So, you are in love with Sabina MacDonnell, the woman I am pledged to wed," he stated quietly.

Brody sank down in the chair and covered his face with both hands. "It doesn't matter. If the two of you do not marry, we will be at war and the people we love will die. I will not be the cause of it. My feelings are unimportant when it comes to the bigger picture."

"I disagree, little brother," said Colin, his voice full of

compassion and understanding as he poured two large glasses. He eyed him warily and slid the glass across the table. "Did you deflower her?"

Brody snatched the glass, downed it, and refused to look Colin in the eye.

"So, that would be another 'yes'," he said, dryly and pushed his cup aside. "Well, this will be an awkward beginning to my marriage, won't it?"

"I beg your forgiveness!" said Brody. "I never meant for this to happen, but when I met her, I could not help but fall in love with her, even though I knew it was wrong. Please, don't hate me."

Colin folded his arms and rested them on the desk. "Don't be ridiculous. It's not like she is a woman I have feelings for. If truth be told, marrying her is the last thing I want to do."

"How did you find out?" asked Brody, as he wiped a bead of sweat from his brow. "We made it a point to be very discreet."

"You wouldn't believe me if I told you. I am not even sure I do." He refilled Brody's glass and picked up his own. "The real question is, what are we going to do now, especially since I have fallen in love with another?"

"You? In love?" Brody sputtered. "Since when?"

Colin chuckled softly. "God help me! Since Willow Mason dropped into my life out of nowhere nearly two weeks ago."

"Well, we are a fine pair, aren't we?" scoffed Brody.

"What we truly are is a FECKED pair," mumbled Colin. "And

not in a good way."

"Here ye are!" The two were nursing another round of whiskey by the time Stewart located them. "Good news, son!" he announced. "A messenger just arrived, and the MacDonnells will be arriving tomorrow. As soon as they have been properly welcomed, we can begin the final preparations for the wedding. I have sent word to yer sister, and she and Finn should be here in time."

Colin and Brody exchanged exasperated looks and drained their glasses.

That evening, Willow sat on the edge of the windowsill watching the sun sink lower in the sky when she heard a knock on the door. "Come in!" she called out.

"Am I disturbing you?" Colin asked and closed the door behind him.

"Not at all!" she smiled over her shoulder. "I was just enjoying the view."

He came to stand behind her and looked up into the sky. "I sometimes forget to appreciate the small wonders of this world like the sunset," he said.

"In my time, there are so many buildings and lights it is hard to even see much of nature, but here, you have the perfect view."

"Yes, I do," he said quietly as he looked down at her.

He walked toward the fireplace. "While I am having a hard time accepting you are not from here, so far, everything else you have told me has turned out to be true."

"You spoke with Brody and he confirmed it, I assume?" she asked and limped over to him.

He pulled a chair around for her and helped her to sit. "He did, not that it matters. I must still wed her."

"Even after all I have told you?"

He knelt and took her hand. "If I do not, I know people will die, but with the information you have given me, if we know what is to happen before it does, we can prevent it. I will simply make sure the marriage is a true marriage in every sense after Brody leaves. It would not be right to force him to live under the same roof while I am married to the woman he loves."

"Whoa!" Willow held up her free hand. "You mean, you will—"

"Knowing from you how anxious her father is to let a war happen, I will not give him any reason to start one. I will be a devoted husband and make arrangements to keep her a faithful wife. Brody has agreed to go to the northern part of the region for an extended period of time to give me a chance to woo her and, perhaps in his absence, it will give her a chance to become at least amicable toward our marriage."

"And if she doesn't, you will be stuck in a loveless marriage for the rest of your life."

He stroked her hand with his fingers. "It is a small price to pay to see my family and the people here safe."

A numbness crept over Willow; she felt like she had been punched in the gut. She wasn't sure what to think. Maybe she had done exactly all that was needed of her and the battle had been prevented. Maybe her mission was complete, and somehow, she would be sent home, but she did not relish the thought, for Colin would no longer be in either of her worlds. The thought made her feel an emptiness that overwhelmed everything else, catching her off guard.

"They are arriving tomorrow," she heard him say, "and the wedding preparations will begin. We will be married shortly thereafter."

Willow swallowed hard as she tried to keep it together on the outside, but on the inside, she was being ripped apart. "I see," she said.

"Will you dine with me tonight in my private chamber?" he asked suddenly. "We may not get many more chances to be alone before then."

"No other whores available for the night?" she remarked snidely, but he gripped her hand so tightly, she flinched.

"I would never think of you in such a way, and I do not wish to be with anyone else," he said softly. He cleared his throat. "Please, Willow! I will be waiting for you. I hope you will come."

Colin left the room and, after he closed the door, he leaned his forehead against it as a few tears fell. He silently prayed she would come to him. He had not known her long, but it was long enough to know he needed this woman more than anything else in the world. His heart was breaking, and it was killing him inside to know he must marry another.

Willow dropped her head back on the chair. She was still reeling from the new turn of events, and it did not sit well with her. "Okay, King of Fae and Fates," she called out, "if I have done all I am meant to do, then send me back to the future. If this is what you wanted, then my work is done, and you can pop me right back to 2016—anytime now—to my cheating boyfriend—and my empty bed—and my floundering store—and my dwindling bank account—" The more she said it aloud, the worse it sounded. When she received no response, she lifted her head, shrugged and giggled. "I suppose that is a sign I need to stay, and I have a couple of days left to stop this wedding." Maybe, just maybe, if she played her cards right, she could convince him to call the whole thing off, but she would need a little assistance.

She slipped downstairs and located the kitchen—and Molly. "Did ye need something, dear?"

Willow wrung her hands. "Colin wants me to have supper with

him tonight in his room."

Molly grinned up from the pot she was stirring on the fire. "Well now, he doesn't usually dine with his nightly visitors. I guess ye must be something special! What can ole Molly do to help?"

"A bath with some of that lavender soap?" she asked hopefully.

Molly touched her arm. "I will get it up to yer room right now." She stepped back and looked Willow up and down as she pondered something. "Ye know what, I have a little something else in mind to make yer evening a little more interesting. Go on up and wait for me."

Half an hour later, Molly had a tub filled by several of the servants, waiting ready in the room.

"I've got one more thing for ye," she said and laid out a beautiful red silk gown on the bed. It wasn't like the other ones because the fabric was fine enough to cling to her body in all the right places. "Ye put this on, and he will be following ye around like a lost puppy the way his father did when he saw his mother in it. He will forget all about the MacDonnell lass in no time."

"It's beautiful!" she smiled and embraced her. "Thanks, Molly!"

Molly hugged her back and left her alone to bathe.

10

CHAPTER TEN

Colin paced nervously, stopping to ensure all the candles were lit, the food was ready, and the fire had plenty of wood. He was starting to think she wasn't coming after all and was about to go to her room to look for her when he heard a soft knock. He took one last look around before opening the door and smiled—the expression on his face said it all.

"Dear God, you are the most beautiful creature I have ever laid eyes upon in my entire life," he said as he stared at her adoringly.

"Are you going to invite me inside or make me wait out here in the hall all night?" she asked with a smirk.

He shook himself. "Of course! Please, come in," and he stepped aside. He closed the door and led her over to a small table he had brought in for the occasion, along with two chairs. The chamber was illuminated by the fire and at least twenty candles in various nooks and crannies along the wall. The entire scene was nothing short of magical.

He offered her a seat, but she continued to stand. "Aren't you hungry?" he asked.

"I am, but not for food," and she stepped into his arms. Resting her hands flat on his chest, she could feel how fast his heart was beating. He placed one hand on her hip, slowly raised her right hand, and proceeded to suckle on each finger sensually, one by one, his eyes fixated on hers. When he was done with her hand, he moved to her lips, enveloping her greedily. A spark of electricity ignited between them, charging the air around them. Willow suddenly felt lightheaded as if she had left her body and was floating above the floor. She wrapped her arms around his neck as he slid his hands over her bottom. His kiss became more urgent, demanding her full attention, as did hers in return.

"I think it is too hot in here for this dress," she said, breathlessly.

"I can help with that," he said. Slowly, he slipped it off her shoulders, letting it drop into a pool around her on the floor, until she stood bare before him. He took a moment to drink in her beauty before he swept her up in his arms and gently laid her across his bed. Colin joined her and took his time teasing and nibbling on one breast and then the other before dropping his head lower, tracing a line down her body with his tongue. He lifted her legs onto his shoulders and settled in. Licking her outer petals, he teased her at first, then suckled before burying his tongue deep within her most intimate recesses. She moaned, clutched his hair, and called out his name as the momentum built;

he refused to relinquish his hold until she had peaked and shattered into a million pieces. As her body continued to shudder, he nuzzled her lovingly and covered her apex with even more kisses.

When he looked up and smiled at her, she pulled his head up to hers urgently while tearing at his shirt. He raised and unbuckled his belt, his kilt falling away. Willow sighed when she saw him in all his glory, resigning herself to the fact that no other man in the world would ever satisfy her after being with him.

"Have you ever been with a man?" he asked, his eyelids heavy, his mind and body burdened with desire.

"Not one like you!" Gripping his hips with her hands, she pulled him toward her.

He closed his eyes and hissed through his teeth, "I need you more than I need the air I breathe, Willow Mason!" before pressing the tip of his throbbing arousal to her opening, clearing the way and filling her with one powerful, all-encompassing stroke. She cried out and he instantly froze, afraid to move. "Am I hurting you?" he demanded, his voice strained and his eyes wide with concern.

"NO!" she shouted and wrapped her legs around him. "Don't stop! Don't EVER stop, especially at this point!" Tossing his head back, he laughed before slowly beginning to move in and out, taking his time, teasing her at first to let her adjust to his size. He began to move faster until she reached another summit, arching her back and tightening around him. He pumped harder and with more speed, until the only sound to be heard was the sound of skin upon skin, the fulfillment of his own need now his only focus, until he felt himself about to come undone. Finally, he cried out and released as he buried his seed deep inside her. He kissed her lips and rested his head on her breast long enough to catch his breath before he rolled onto his side and pulled her over onto his chest. "God help me!" he whispered as he gazed up and intertwined his fingers with hers, "All is lost for I have fallen completely in love with you."

She shifted to look up at him as he stroked her arm. "You love me?"

"More than anyone or anything in this world!"

She smiled. "As absolutely batshit crazy as it sounds, I feel the same way!"

He slowly made love to her twice more and, when morning came, they lay happily sated and entangled in one another's arms, Willow now convinced she had changed his mind. They woke when someone banged loudly on the door. "The MacDonnells are here!" called his father. "Get dressed and come to greet yer bride."

Colin sighed heavily and pushed back the covers.

"What are you going to do?" she asked.

He kissed her thoroughly and stared deeply into her eyes as he stroked her cheek, his face full of wretched misery. "I am going to meet my bride," he said and sat up on the edge of the bed.

She raised up with the blanket pulled to cover her breasts. "What?" she asked in disbelief. "But you said you loved me, and you needed me! I don't understand!"

"And I do," he declared sincerely and full of love, "but that does not release me from my obligations as Laird of this land." He reached over and grasped her hand. "I will purchase a house for you in the village and provide everything you need. You will never want for anything, and any children we are blessed with from our love will be well-cared for and adored by both their parents."

Willow snatched her hand back. "You want me to be your mistress? Your whore on the side you intend to sneak in and out to see when it is convenient for you?"

"Never refer to yourself in such a manner!" he growled. His face darkened as he stood. "You are the only one I love and the only one I truly want to be with."

He put on his shirt and pulled his tartan around his waist.

"And if I refuse?" she asked, scornfully.

He fastened his belt and sat back down on the bed. "That would certainly be your choice, but I beg you, please don't, because it will break my heart. I would give you everything, and more if I only could, but I am simply not in a position to. You are the one who told me my actions will determine the fate of these people I watch over and love, and I cannot fail them, no matter how painful the cost." He leaned to kiss her, but she turned her face away.

Colin dropped his head, wiped his nose on his sleeve, and got up to leave.

"I will return as soon as I am able. Please, wait here for me," he said and left.

Once he was gone, Willow curled on her side, pulled her knees up to her chest, and cried.

When no more tears were left to fall, she forced herself to get up and dress. When she started out of the room toward her own, she heard the sounds of a large group of people gathered in the hall. Slipping down the staircase to see what was happening, she stealthily blended into the crowd. Colin stood at the fireplace in the main hall with his father on one side and, who she assumed was his brother, on the other, as a group of people made their way up the center and stopped when they reached Colin.

"Laird MacLeod, we thank ye for yer hospitality. I am Aenghus MacDonnell. Allow me to present my daughter, and your bride, Sabina." A young woman, no more than nineteen, with large brown eyes and dark hair stepped forward, her head bent down.

Colin smiled, took Sabina by the hand, and dropped to his knee. "You do me a great honor by agreeing to be my wife," he said and kissed her hand. When he stood, he instantly took notice of Willow in the crowd, and she watched as the breath went out of his body as he locked eyes with her.

She closed her eyes, turned away, and rushed out of the room.

"Shall we break bread?" Colin asked and held out his hand in the direction of the dining hall. He stepped backward and spoke a few words to Brody, who then excused himself and went in the other direction. Stewart cut his son a hostile look, but Colin warned him off with a stern, resolute one of his own in return.

Willow found herself outside, sucking in air, as she tried to keep herself from falling apart. She walked until she reached Mary's resting place and sat down on the bench with her face in her hands and a great deal on her mind.

"Will you allow me to escort you to somewhere more private?" a kindly voice asked from just to her right. She looked up to see a man who looked a great deal like Colin, only younger, with his hands folded behind him watching her intently.

"Let me guess—you would be Brody," she said and looked down at the ground.

"I am, and you are Willow." He sat down next to her and his eyes fell on his mother's gravestone. "Colin knew you were upset, and he sent me to check on you."

"Don't you mean he wants to keep his whore out of sight and hidden from his betrothed?" she barked.

Brody scratched his forehead and winced. "That's a little harsh, don't you think?"

Willow turned to glare at him. "So is spending the night with a woman and telling her you love her more than anything else in the world, just before leaving to go meet your soon-to-be wife," she spat.

"This situation is not ideal for anyone," he said quietly.

"That's right!" she snapped her fingers. "Because you are in love with the bride and your soon-to-be sister-in-law. What could possibly go wrong there?"

"He told you?"

"Actually, I told him. I have a gift, if that is what you want to call it, although right now, I consider it a total pain in the ass. All it has done is trap me here and cause me nothing but heartache."

Brody looked around nervously as people started to gather outside. "Please, let's speak somewhere more private."

Willow stood. "I have a better idea. Why don't you tell the Laird his 'problem' is leaving and is going to try and go back to where she came from? He need not concern himself about my welfare any longer. I hope he and his wife are incredibly happy together." She stormed off toward the back of the house.

Colin sat at the head of the table with Sabina at his side. "I hope the meal is to your liking," he said.

"Nothing is to my liking," she said vehemently but smiled in her father's direction. "I hate everything about this place."

"I am sure you will get used to it," offered Colin and sipped from his glass. "I will make things as pleasant as I can for you. I want you to be content here, happy even."

"I will never be content here," she whispered, "And I will never be happy as yer wife. I'd sooner lay with a pig than crawl into yer bed."

Colin choked on his drink and coughed. He took another swallow and wondered exactly what he had gotten himself into.

Colin's father raised his glass. "A toast to the joining of our two families and may yer marriage and children unite us for many generations to come."

Sabina's father lifted his glass. "May the next generation be sired on yer wedding night."

Sabina groaned and looked in the other direction.

Colin drained his cup. He saw Brody headed his way, looking less than successful on his mission, and stood. "Excuse me, I need to see to some affairs of the estate. I will return shortly."

He stepped to the side and Brody whispered in his ear as Colin's eyes went wild. "Damn it!" he said. "Find her and stop her! You cannot let her leave here, no matter what!"

"What am I supposed to do?" he asked in a hushed tone. "Lock her up somewhere?"

"Do whatever it takes!" commanded Colin. "I will NOT lose her!"

Brody shook his head. "I think you need to accept you may already have, brother. You cannot seriously expect her to enthusiastically play your mistress, while another woman lives under your roof and sleeps in your bed, bearing your name and your children. It is asking a bit too much.

His eyes caught sight of Sabina and hers his. They locked eyes momentarily before Brody looked away, his face tortured and full of shame.

Colin cursed under his breath when he took notice. He shook his brother by the shoulder to get his full attention. "Just do something to keep her here until I can figure things out!"

Brody folded his arms. "And where exactly are you going to put Willow? In case you have forgotten, the room she is currently occupying will soon be needed for your wedding night."

Colin wrenched his face, "Damn it! I had forgotten! Find her, take her back to my chamber, and keep her there until I can breakaway to speak with her."

Brody huffed and stomped off as Colin returned to his room full of guests.

An hour later, Willow sat in a chair in Colin's room, fuming, her arms and feet restrained.

Brody looked at her apologetically as he stood before her. "I am so sorry about this, but Colin will have my hide if you leave this castle."

"You have got to be kidding me!" she screeched. "I demand you release me this instant!"

"I can't!" He held one elbow in his palm and chewed on his fingernail. "And you need to be quieter, or I am going to have to gag you. If the wrong person hears, we will have a great deal of trouble on our hands."

Her nose flared. "You wouldn't dare!"

He picked up a rag from the table and dangled it. "I'm afraid I would! Haven't you heard? I'm not a particularly good person. I coveted my brother's intended."

Willow growled at him, causing him to take a step back, taking him off guard, and making him a little concerned by her aggressiveness. She pulled at her restraints and grimaced when she tried to stretch her leg.

Brody sighed and offered her a sympathetic look.

"Would you be more comfortable on the bed? I know your foot must still pain you, and you could at least stretch out and rest it a bit?"

"And make it easier for the Laird to waltz in here and have his way with me when he returns. No thanks! How long do you plan on keeping me here?" Willow seethed.

He pulled up a chair and sat down across from her. "Until Colin can speak with you. He was terribly upset when I told him you were going to leave, and he ordered me to keep you here at all costs. For what it's worth, I can't say I have ever seen him like this over a woman before." He looked her up and down. "Since we may be here a while, pray tell me something. How did you know about me and Sabina?"

"It doesn't matter," she mumbled. "None of it matters anymore."

Brody leaned forward. "My brother is a good man caught in an unfortunate situation. As a Laird, he has a great deal of responsibility for many people on his shoulders, and the burden weighs heavily upon him with every decision he makes. Performing his duty means he does not have the luxury of marrying the one he loves and that is truly the greatest tragedy of all. He has no more choice in the matter than Sabina does as the eldest daughter to another laird."

"If you love Sabina, why don't you marry her?" she asked.

Brody rubbed his jaw. "Our marriage would serve no strategic purpose, and her father couldn't care less about her happiness; she is nothing but a means to an end in his eyes and truthfully, I think it would please him more to see her miserable."

"Marrying you off to a child serves no purpose, either, but it seems it is the plan," she scoffed.

"What are you talking about?"

Willow cocked her head in his direction. "After the wedding, your father is going to announce the happy news. He and MacDonnell have come to the agreement that you and Nahla will be wed."

His face paled. "Sabina's sister? She is but a girl!"

Willow shrugged. "That's what you get when you let other

people make all your decisions for you. So, everyone will be one big unhappy family for the rest of their lives. Forgive me if I don't want to be a part of it. I have already had one man who made me his second choice, and I will never allow it to happen again."

He stared at the floor. "That cannot be right! Why in God's name would they make such an agreement? I know MacDonnell has no love for his daughters because he wanted sons to fight but marrying off his youngest at such a tender age seems a bit much, even for him. How can a man treat his own children in that manner?"

Willow dropped her head back. "Maybe he WANTS them to be unhappy. Some people live for shit like that, and he kills two birds with one stone. He gets whatever he gets in the bargain, and they are out of his hair for good. What is the going price for a daughter these days anyway?"

Brody looked as if the wheels in his head had suddenly started to turn. "He gets a hold in the south for Sabina and will no doubt, ask the same price for Nahla."

Willow frowned. "Wait, I thought the bride's family paid the dowry, so why are the MacLeods the ones giving up land?"

Brody stood. "MacDonnell insisted on a show of good faith, and he refused to agree to it otherwise. Father was so anxious to make the match, he readily accepted."

They both looked up when the door flew open, and Colin came

inside.

"Tired of her already?" snarked Willow. "There was no reason to hurry back when your side piece of ass is TIED UP IN YOUR ROOM!" she roared, furiously.

"You tied her up?" he asked Brody.

"You said to do whatever it took!"

"Oh, dear God!" huffed Colin as he came to her side, but Brody caught him by the arm. "We need to talk."

"What do you mean?"

"Willow says father wants Nahla and I to wed."

Colin sighed. "He has made no mention of it to me."

"He's going to tell you at the wedding!" she said and rolled her eyes.

"I cannot marry Nahla!" exclaimed Brody. "We are already giving up the south keep for your marriage to Sabina. He will no doubt demand the west for Nahla and that will put us at a great disadvantage if things go awry. It is not a position we can afford to put ourselves in. It will leave us too vulnerable."

"I will not allow anyone else to be forced into a marriage they do not desire," assured Colin, firmly. "MacDonnell has gotten all he is getting from us, especially since Father is no longer in charge of these decisions."

Colin tilted his head towards the door, a silent dismissal. Brody acknowledged his brother and immediately departed, closing the door quietly behind him.

Colin knelt before Willow and cupped her face with his hand. She tried to look away, but he held her in place. "I love you, and I cannot be without you. Please, I am on my knees begging you to not leave me. I cannot do this without you."

Tears sprang to her eyes. "And I cannot allow myself to be second best for any man. Ronnie, the man I was with in the future, used me and took another woman on the side. He fucked her, and an hour later was trying to do the same to me. If I become your mistress, every time we are together, I will think of nothing but you being in her arms and in her bed. I will always wonder if you just fucked her mere moments before coming to me. I have too much respect for myself to ever live like that again, no matter how much I love you."

"Give me some time to figure this out," he whispered, pitifully. "PLEASE!"

"You have already made your decision, and it means I have also made mine," she said. "Please untie me."

He reluctantly pulled a dirk from his boot and cut her loose. She rubbed her wrists once they were free and looked into his eyes. She pulled his face to hers and kissed him. "I have to leave now," she choked out.

"Where will you go? If everything you have told me is true, you have no one to go to for help, no money, and no roof over your head. Do you have any idea what could happen to you if you leave the safety of this castle? Do you know what men will do to you if you are caught out alone?"

"I do, and whatever happens to me cannot possibly be worse than seeing you with another woman," she whispered and left the room.

Willow made it back to her room before completely breaking down. She had no idea what she was going to do. The King of the Fae seemed to be ignoring her calls, which meant she was stuck in 1585. She didn't know where to go, had no way to support herself, or even any idea of where to start. She only knew it hurt too much to stay where she was. She put on the shoes Colin had brought up for her, even though her foot was still very painful, took one last look around, wiped her face with her hand, and left.

Once Willow was outside, she focused on her surroundings to get her bearings. She started in the direction of the village but moved slowly because of the worsening ache in her foot. It looked to be about a mile away and was just outside the walls of the castle; strange to see now because the enclosure did not exist in the future.

She made it about halfway there before the pain from her foot in the shoe became overwhelming and she had to stop to rest. Leaning against a large boulder, she removed the slipper, only to see her foot was swelling again and, as if that wasn't bad enough, it had started to rain.

"Oh, come on!" she shouted to the sky and started off again, wrapping her arms around herself for warmth because she had not had the foresight to bring a cloak. By the time Willow reached the village, she was soaking wet, chilled to the bone, and in an enormous amount of pain. At least she had some time to clear her mind a bit and had come up with a plan of sorts as she walked. Maybe she could find someone who worshipped the old gods, a pagan or a druid, and see if they knew of a way to reach out to this King of the Fae. If so, perhaps she could find a way home.

As much as she didn't want to leave Colin, she refused to be kept on the side while he married another. If Ronnie taught her one thing, it was she deserved better. There had to be somebody out there who knew how to contact this 'Fae' guy. The first place she came to was a tavern and the smell of cooking food made her stomach growl. It also made her realize she had been foolish enough to leave without breakfast and had not eaten since the mid-day meal the day before because she and Colin had not gotten around to it. But as hungry as she was, she had no money and nothing to trade. "Alright, Willow. Maybe you rushed out a little prematurely and didn't quite think this through," she chided herself.

Standing in the now pouring rain, trying to decide what to do next, the door to the tavern flew open and a woman waved her in. "Yer gonna catch yer death out there. Get in here, lass!"

She didn't have to be told twice and rushed inside. "Go on over by the fireplace and warm yerself," said the kindly, older lady.

"Thank you!" she said and wobbled over, shivering from the cold to sit at the table closest to the fire. The woman brought her over something warm to drink as she rubbed her hands together. "I can't accept this. I don't have any money," she said and pushed it away.

"First one's on me," the lady said with a warm smile. "I am Bridget, by the way, and ye look like ye have had a rough day."

"I'm Willow, and I suppose I have. It's what happens when you are stupid enough to fall in love with the Laird who is betrothed to another," she muttered as she warmed her hands on the cup.

"That'll do it!" The woman grinned and patted her gently on the arm.

Willow smiled up at her. "Thank you again."

Bridget rubbed her shoulder and went back to clearing off tables.

Looking around the room, Willow saw she was the only woman at the tables, which made her slouch down, hoping to go unnoticed. As Bridget went to fill the cups of three men in the corner, Willow noticed the tavern keep was being followed around by a small, scrawny older man trying desperately to get her attention. When he noticed Willow was watching him, he rushed over to the table. "Can ye see me?"

She nodded, her eyes darting around to see if anyone was paying her any mind.

"Oh, thank goodness! I have been trying to speak with my sweet Bridget for weeks now, but I can't get through to her."

Willow tucked her head down and raised the cup as to not be noticed while she spoke. "Do you know you have passed?"

He sat down at the table. "Aye, I do, but I need to tell my wife something especially important. Can ye do it for me? Please?"

"I would be happy to. What is it?" she asked.

"Tell her I hid the money we saved in a cask in the storeroom. She needs it to keep this place going and to take care of our boy. It's marked 'port' because no self-respecting Scot would ever steal that!" He laughed.

"I will tell her. Anything else?"

"Aye! Tell her I love her, and I miss her verra much."

Willow nodded. "I'll take care of it."

"Thank ye, lass. I am in yer debt."

"One thing," Willow stopped him before he disappeared. "Do you by chance know anyone who might be able to contact the Fae King?" she asked hopefully.

He frowned and scratched his head in thought. "That's old magic, lass, and the ones who practice it tend to keep to themselves, but I can tell ye one thing. According to the stories my granny used to tell, he won't bother with ye even if ye find someone with the power to summon him unless he WANTS to speak to ye. The Fae King answers to no mortal, and ye will only be wasting yer time. If he has business with ye, he will make it a point to find ye."

Willow pushed the wet hair away from her face. "Thanks, anyway. Go rest in peace and enjoy your afterlife," she smiled, and he slowly faded from her eyes.

Willow waved Bridget over. "Ye need something dear?"

"No, but you do," whispered Willow. "I don't know how to say this without sounding like a person who is unwell in the head, so I am just going to say it. Your husband said to tell you he loves you, and the money is hidden in the storeroom in a cask marked 'port'."

Bridget paled as she slowly sat down on the bench next to her. "Is this some sort of joke? Are ye a witch?"

"No, I am not!" Willow shook her head. "Just go check. He wants to make sure you find it so you and your son are taken care of."

Bridget looked toward the back, wiped her mouth, and got up. She returned a short time later with a bowl of stew and placed it in front of Willow. "Ye look like ye could use a hot meal, and I can afford to give ye one now." She sat down next to her. "How did ye know?"

Willow took a bite of the glorious smelling stew and moaned. "I have a gift and can see those who have left this life. If they have messages, I just pass them along."

"Is he alright?" she asked, softly.

"He is, but he misses you."

Bridget wiped her eyes with a towel. "I lost my dear sweet man nearly a month ago and I feel like part of my soul went with him. I had no idea how I was going to care for our son without the money. Thank ye, lass!" she said.

"I am glad I could help someone."

Bridget used the towel thrown over her shoulder to wipe down the table. "What's this business about ye and the Laird?"

Willow shrugged. "Oh! I am afraid that story doesn't have a happy ending. He said he loved me but had to marry someone else. He asked me to be his mistress, and I turned him down. The end." She looked over at Bridget. "But, then again, I got to meet a nice lady and enjoy a bowl of her wonderful stew, so maybe it has a happy ending after all."

"Well, ye will always have a hot meal here whenever ye like it!" she said and went back to work.

Willow finished her food, set her dish aside, and folded her arms on the table. She sat there for nearly half an hour just enjoying the warmth of the fire and a full belly. "Now what do I do?" she asked herself as she laid her head down and closed her eyes for a moment, trying to forget about the pain in her foot.

"If ye need a warm, dry place to lay down lass, I can help ye with that!" she heard a man say. "I have a nice bed ye can stay in and keep me company in more ways than one."

Willow sighed and looked up. "Thank you for the kind offer," she replied sarcastically, "but I think I will pass."

"Oh, she's English," said another as he came over. "I always wondered what it would be like to feck an Englishwoman!" He smirked wickedly as he sat down next to her. "They say ye English women are uptight, especially where it counts. I can't wait to find out if it's true."

She shrank away from him but felt the hand of a third man who had come up on her other side firmly on her back.

"Get off of me!" She jerked away from his touch.

"Ye don't have to be like that, lass," said the first man. "If ye don't fight too hard, ye just might like it. I will go first and get ye good and ready for my two friends. Ye see, the three of us, we share everything."

The second man grabbed her by the wrist. "I kind of like it when they fight!" he sneered and dug his ragged fingernails into her arm.

Willow now realized why Colin didn't want her away from the safety of the castle walls. Men were different in this time and not in a good way. She managed to stand up and tried to free herself from his grip, when the third man snaked his arms around her waist and picked her up off the floor, leaving her feet dangling in the air.

"Let go of me!" she screamed and kicked.

"We will let ye go when we are done with ye, but this might

take a while," said the first man as he pulled at the bodice of her dress and ripped it open, before the third man, who still held her, dropped her flat on her back on the bench, banging the back of her head hard on the wood in the process. He then pulled her gown up, around her waist, and held her down for the first man who had already roughly shoved her knees apart. Smiling cruelly, he untied his breeches and planted himself between her legs, before taking his erection in hand and closing in on his goal. Dizzy and disoriented, Willow tried to scream, but the man holding her down covered her mouth with his dirty, calloused hand, preventing her.

Suddenly, the first man was gone. He had been thrown back against the wall and landed with a 'thud' in a heap. The second man's face met the top of the table three times before he lay bloody and unmoving on the floor, and the third man went straight through one of the glass windows.

Willow lay unmoving on the bench, breathing hard as her mind tried to process what was happening. Someone went to pick her up in his arms, and she instinctively fought back with everything she had in her.

"Willow! It's me! It's Colin!" he said when she looked up. She stopped struggling and burst into tears as he pulled her tightly to him. "You are safe! I am here now! No one is ever going to hurt you again."

He wrapped her up in a blanket Bridget brought over, picked

her up, and carried her to the door the tavern owner held open for him. "Thank you for sending your son to let me know she was here, Bridget. I will pay for the damages to your window, and I will make sure those three never darken your door again."

"I am only glad ye got here in time. I had a strange feeling they were going to be trouble when they crossed the threshold. Ye just make sure ye take care of that lass!" she smiled. "She is very special!"

"Yes, she is," he whispered.

He carried her outside, placed her on his horse, and climbed into the saddle behind her.

"How badly are you hurt?" he asked as he tucked the blanket around her protectively and pulled her tightly to him.

"I'm okay, I think," she said in a shaky voice as her body trembled uncontrollably.

"I told you it was not safe. I should have never let you out of my sight," he fussed as he spurred the horse forward. He buried his face in her hair as Willow silently cried, and they rode full gallop back to the castle. When they reached home, he helped her down from the saddle and carried her to her room.

After he deposited her in a chair by the fire, he wrapped a dry blanket around her, poured a whiskey, and made her drink it all down.

He located a clean rag, brought a bowl of water over to where she was, and gently cleaned the cuts on her face and the gouges on her arms in silence as she sat with a blank expression. When he was done, Colin took her face in his hands and tenderly said, "Change your clothes, get warm and rest. I have some matters to attend to, but I will be back as soon as I can. Know what I do from here on is for the best, and it is because I love you." He kissed her forehead and left.

As soon as he reached the door, Willow heard the distinct sound of the lock being turned. She ran to it and pulled at the door, but it did not budge. She banged on it with her hand.

"Colin! Don't lock me in here!"

"I'm sorry," she heard him say from the other side. "This is for your own good."

"Colin! You cannot keep me here against my will!" she shouted.

"You will remain here until I can make arrangements for your safety. You will be under my protection even if you choose not to be with me. I love you too much to let anything happen to you." She listened to his footsteps as he walked away.

She screamed out in frustration, smacked the door with her hand, and slid down to the floor, only to burst into tears again.

Colin made it into his room before his knees buckled and almost gave way from beneath him. He forced himself over to the table and downed several large gulps of whiskey before he was able to sufficiently compose himself.

Willow had run off, nearly getting herself raped and killed in the process. Thank God Bridget had sent her son to find him when she showed up, and he had arrived just in time. Another moment and those bastards would have done irreparable physical and mental damage to the woman he loved. If anything had happened to her, he would have never forgiven himself and he knew, in that moment, he could never be without her, no matter how steep the price.

It was late evening when she heard the door open. She sat up in the bed where she had been wrapped up in a quilt since they returned and watched as Colin brought in a tray.

"It occurred to me you might be hungry," he said sheepishly. She stared blankly past him as he put it on the table next to the bed and sat down, rubbing his hands together nervously. "I want to apologize for locking you in here. In truth, I just panicked when I saw you—what almost happened—and when I saw those men attacking you—" he stopped to compose himself and clear his throat when his voice cracked. "I do understand when I asked you to stay with me, it was too much to ask, but I did not think you would endanger yourself by running away from me. You said the man you were with in the future used you, and that is not something I ever want you to believe of me." He stood, raked back his hair, and paced the floor. "I have decided to call off the wedding."

"What?" She slowly looked up at him. "I thought you couldn't. What about—" she started.

"To hell with the consequences!" he interrupted. "If it costs me my life, then so be it. One more night with you is worth a thousand deaths, and if one last time is all I am permitted in this world, then so be it."

She scooted up to the edge of the bed. "What about all of the people here?"

He folded his arms and shrugged. "Perhaps, I can give MacDonnell something else he wants more and that, along with offering up my life—maybe it will be enough to send him away without hurting anyone."

She went to him and took his hand. "I will not allow you to give up your life for me," she said and leaned into him.

He put his arms around her and pulled her against him. "I would do anything for you, and my life is a small price to pay for you to be safe!" He kissed the top of her head.

"There has to be another way!" she said.

He pushed her back a bit. "Eat, regain your strength, and spend the night with me? Please?"

She nodded.

"I have to go tend to a couple of things quickly. Come to my room when you are ready." He took her face in his hands, kissed her tenderly, and left to take care of his business.

Willow crawled onto the bed and picked at her food as she thought about the situation. There had to be a solution; she just needed to figure out what it was. She had come too far to watch him die now.

As she pondered the impossible situation, Mary suddenly appeared on the bed next to her with her finger pressed to her lips while shushing her. Pointing toward the door, she motioned for Willow to quietly follow her over.

Willow furrowed her brow, puzzled, and carefully crawled off the bed. She noticed Colin had left the door slightly ajar and when she got to it, she heard whispering just outside. Mary indicated she should listen closely to the conversation and vanished as quickly as she came. Willow realized the voices belonged to Sabina and her little sister, it being obvious they thought the end of the hall a safe place to speak.

"What am I going to do, Nahla? My courses are more than a week late, and I am fairly certain I am with child."

"Ye will be married tomorrow," said Nahla, innocently. "Everyone will just think it is his child conceived on your wedding night."

"But it won't be his. It will be his brother's," fretted Sabina.

"No one will know. The babe will be raised a MacLeod and that is all that matters," assured Nahla. "And since it will be clear soon ye are with child, the husband ye despise will never need to touch ye again. There are worse ways to live, as we both well know. At least ye will be away from our father."

Sabina's voice became strained. "I just don't want to marry him. I have fallen in love with Brody, and I will never want to share a bed with another. He is so sweet and kind, nothing like Colin. The thought of having to be with the Laird makes me want to run away."

Nahla embraced her sister. "Listen to me! Ye must put Brody out of yer mind and be a good and obedient wife to your betrothed. Father will kill ye if he thinks ye are anything but dutiful, and I cannot bear to lose my big sister. Ye have to forget about Brody."

Sabina touched Nahla's face. "I will do my best if only to keep ye from having to become the Laird's wife in my place. I have heard from the women in this village of his ferocious lust, and I will do anything to protect ye from having to endure him. I promised Mother I would look after ye, and it is what I intend to do."

The sisters hugged once more and moved away when they heard voices nearby.

"Wow!" Willow mouthed to herself and waited for them to leave before she checked the hall and slipped down to Colin's room. She was sitting on the bed cross-legged, with one of his tartans wrapped around her when he returned.

"I am delighted you are here," he smiled sweetly as he closed the door and bolted it.

"We need to talk," she said and patted the bed.

His smile faded to a frown as he strode across the floor. "Are you alright?" he asked worriedly, cupping her face as he looked her over. "Are you unwell, or more injured than I realized?" Do you need the healer?"

Willow shook her head and laid her hand over his. "No, I am fine. This is about something else."

"What is it, my love?"

She blew out a deep breath. "I just overheard Sabina tell Nahla she is fairly certain she carries Brody's baby."

Colin's face clouded over with disbelief and his jaw dropped in astonishment. "You are certain?"

"She seems to be. How long has it been since Brody went there?"

"Originally? About five weeks."

Willow made a face. "Yeah, that would be about right if he got her pregnant when they first got together."

"What a mess!" he said as he took off his boots and crawled on the bed next to her. "Her father very well may have Brody's balls on his breakfast plate right next to mine."

"Although, if there is a child, he may let you off the hook," she said hopefully.

"It doesn't matter either way," he said as he turned on his side to face her. "She is betrothed to the Laird of the MacLeod clan." He decided it was time to focus all his attention on her. "I will worry about that tomorrow. Right now, the condemned one has one final request, and you are the only one who can fulfill it. If you are feeling up to it and, more importantly, would like to spend the night with me, I would be an extremely fortunate soul if you allowed me to make love to you until dawn. If you are not, I would be equally happy to have you lie here in my arms, talking and keeping me company until morning. Either way, I will have the memory of a perfect night with the woman I love to carry into the next world."

Willow looked deeply into his eyes. "I love you, Colin MacLeod, and if we only have one more night together, I want it to be a memorable one." She leaned forward and pressed her lips to his.

He kissed her adoringly, relishing each moment in her arms as if they were indeed his last. He undressed her slowly, taking the time to touch each part of her skin, committing every inch of her to his memory. When he had finished, he relieved himself of his clothing and they lay facing each other with nothing between them.

Willow rolled on top of him and straddled him as she took her time tasting every inch of his delicious chest, circling his nipples with her fingertips, before shifting her body and moving her attention a little bit lower. She licked and teased his already swollen shaft as she cupped his balls in her palm, lightly kneading them before dropping her head down further to gently graze one and then the other with her teeth.

He let out a groan of euphoric bliss when she unexpectedly took his manhood fully into her mouth in one quick move, formed a tight seal with her lips, and suckled his rigid shaft so hard his hips lifted from the bed as he let out a sound of pure exhilaration.

She caught sight of him looking down at her when he placed his hand on the back of her head, and the burning desire on his face made her take notice of her own desperate need. Willow smiled and closed in tighter with her lips, moving in a steady up and down bob, almost pushing him completely over the edge, and causing him to close his eyes while calling out her name—in a state of jubilant torture as he fought to control himself.

When he could hold back no more, he firmly grasped her arms and pulled her up, so they were face to face. "I need to be a part of you NOW!" he hissed through his teeth.

She obliged him by positioning herself over his massive member and slowly working the tip of his erection back and forth in a sensual tease against her slick, wet heat.

When he felt how ready she was for him, he placed his hands on her hips and plunged himself into her sweetness, burying himself to the hilt. He thrust upwards, holding himself there in place until she adjusted, steadied herself, and braced her hands on his chest. As he began to move, she met his vigor with her own, slowly at first until they settled into a beautiful, steady rhythm that ended in an explosion of ecstasy leaving them both in a state of undeniable bliss.

"God, I love you!" he panted as he wrapped his arms around her; she collapsed against his chest as he covered her in kisses.

"Too bad our timing sucks!" she said.

"Actually, I think our timing was perfect," he retorted with a sly grin.

"You know what I mean," she smiled with the side of her face pressed against his chest.

"What's it like in the future?" he asked as he stroked her hair.

"Well, this place has gone downhill a bit," she replied.

He rolled her onto her side, so they faced each other. "What do you mean?"

"The castle is nothing like this in the future, unfortunately. With none of your family left to take care of it, it falls into a state of disrepair, and they try to keep it up by renting out rooms."

"Well, perhaps we have changed that. Maybe, I will be the only one to die instead of everyone here, and if it is the case, then it will be a good day," he said sadly, linking his fingers with hers, as she settled against his chest.

"Don't say that!"

"I need you to promise me if I do not survive the week and, if I have by some miracle, left you with child, you will try to go back to your time and raise our son or daughter as a MacLeod, so I will know something of me survives in this world and in the future. If you cannot return, I have made arrangements for you to be well provided for so you will never have to worry about anything."

Her eyes welled with tears; he felt them drop upon his chest. He raised her face to his and wiped them with his thumb. "None of that! Whatever happens tomorrow will happen, but tonight is ours, and I want to carry this memory into the next life. Your tears are not what I want to remember."

He kissed her fervently and spent the rest of the night making love to her.

11

CHAPTER ELEVEN

When Willow woke the next morning, Colin was already gone.

She quickly found her clothes, dressed, and snuck out of his room, and down the stairs. There was shouting coming from the room that was the library in the future. Her stomach dropped. He was going to sacrifice himself for her, even if it meant forfeiting his life. She loved him too much to let him do that and decided, then and there, she would do whatever it took to keep him safe.

Willow inched her way closer to the door and was about to burst in when a woman with her hands on her hips appeared in front of her. "Who are you and what are you doing?" she demanded.

"I'm nobody!" she said and started to go around her. The woman grabbed the back of her gown and stopped her. "I know everyone here, and I don't know you. What is your name?"

She sighed and turned back around. "My name is Willow Mason."

The corner of the woman's mouth twitched up. "So, you are the one who has stolen my brother's heart and caused all of this trouble."

Willow should have known. They shared the same smile, the same one they all had and the one exactly like their mother's. It had to be his sister.

As the arguing got louder, his sister took her by the arm and pulled her into the dining hall. "I am Skye, by the way. It is nice to meet you. Are you hungry?"

Willow wrung her hands while glancing nervously over her shoulder. "Is it going to be my last meal?"

"I doubt it!" Skye waved her hand. "Colin's a smart boy, and I am sure he has things well in hand. Let's leave them to sort it out." She sat her down and it wasn't long before Molly came in with a plate.

"Good morning to ye," she said and leaned down to whisper. "Nice work, lass. I think the wedding is officially off."

"Yeah, but at what cost," mumbled Willow.

Skye sat down across from her and watched her closely, with a gleam in her big green eyes. "There is no one by the name of Mason around here. Where did you come from, or did you just fall from the sky?"

"Something like that," Willow muttered, and took a bite of food even though her stomach was in knots, worried about what was happening next door.

"Well, I am going to have to know everything about you, Willow Mason. There must be something special about you to have Colin in such a state."

Skye's face split into a wide grin and she turned her attention to the doorway. "Hello, my love!" she said as a very handsome older man came over and kissed her.

"Good morning, sunshine," he beamed back. "What is all the fuss in the hall about?"

Skye nodded across the table. "Meet Willow, the cause of all the fuss and the woman who has stolen my engaged brother's heart. This is my husband, Finn."

Willow coughed and sputtered. "YOU are Finn?"

"That I am," he bowed and pulled out a chair next to his wife.

"Oh, you and I need to talk, mister," she said and pointed her fork at him.

Skye looked back and forth between the two of them. "What did you do now, lover?" she teased. "We only arrived last evening, and you have not been here long enough to stir up any trouble, well not much anyway."

"I am innocent!" He raised his hands. "I have no idea what I have done, but I am anxious to find out. Please, do tell," he said and smiled at her—and what a smile it was. The man was older, but there was something about him that made him appear younger, and there was an odd warmth rolling off him making her like him instantly.

Willow laid her fork down and placed her arms on the table. "What do you know about the King of Fae and Fates?" she asked.

Skye burst into laughter. "Oh, someone who wants to hear one of your stories. I will leave you to it and go check on things in the other room." He pulled her over for a long, leisurely kiss and to gaze into her eyes. As she stood up, he said, "I love ye!"

"I love you, too!" she purred.

"That woman is my world," he said as he watched her go. Once they were alone, he turned and smiled. "Now, what story would ye like to hear, my dear?"

Willow sighed. "Hmm—the one beginning with a four-hundred-year-old ghost of a laird trapped in a castle, much like this one," she presented her hands over her head, "after an unusual little rhyme was said to him as he lay dying, and it ends with a woman dropping out of the sky into 1585 to stop the slaughter of the MacLeod family."

He scratched his neatly trimmed beard. "I don't believe I know that one, although it does sound intriguing. Please, do tell it to me! I love a good story!"

"Let me see if I can refresh your memory because I recall the poem very clearly—'To one who beholds what others cannot see, I send forth this call across time and seas, with a kiss that touches no mortal lips, a scale from the past will soon be tipped, state your desire plain and clear, for the King of Fae and Fates to hear, your heart will help to lead the way and bring about a better day'.'"

He clapped his hands. "My goodness, ye have a wonderful gift for rhyme! I am impressed!"

She leaned across the table. "That was recited by a man, one who resembles you a great deal, who said he could not bear to see his wife so upset over the death of her entire family and that man's name, oddly enough was Finn. How do I reach the King of Fae and Fates, Finn?"

Finn folded his hands and rested them on the table. "My dear, ye speak of a glorious mythical being unseen by humans for generations. How on Earth would I know? Although, I am curious," he leaned forward, "if ye were to reach out to him, what exactly would ye want of him?" he asked with an impish curl of the lips.

Willow sat back in her chair and thought hard, but her concentration was broken by Colin's bellowing as he stomped into the room.

"My decision is made, and it is FINAL! Determine the damages so we may discuss payment!" He smiled at her when he saw Willow and came over to kiss her on the cheek. "Good morning, my love," he said sweetly.

"Is it?" she winced.

"Don't ye walk away from me!" shouted Aenghus MacDonnell as he and Stewart stormed in. "Ye have insulted me, and my family name by backing out of this bargain! I will not stand for it!"

Colin calmly pulled out the chair next to Willow and sat down. "Bring my breakfast!" he called out to Molly before he turned to Aenghus. "Your daughter would rather lay with a pig than me. She made that perfectly clear, so why would I wed a woman who might slit my throat in my sleep? It is simply not good business."

Aenghus MacDonnell glared at Willow. "Is this the cunt ye choose to take over my daughter?"

Colin slammed his fist on the table. "You will not speak of her that way, and certainly not in my presence. You are a guest in my home. You would do well to remember that and address her with respect!"

"I don't bow to whores!" spat Aenghus.

"I'm not the pregnant virgin bride," mumbled Willow into her hand.

"Oh!" Finn chuckled when he heard her words. His eyes lit up as he looked at Aenghus, an excited grin on his face. "This all just got very interesting! I can't wait to see how it ends."

Stewart went around the table to Colin's other side. "Ye cannot do this! Ye are jeopardizing everything we have worked for! Ye are my son, and ye will do as ye are told!"

Colin's face darkened. "You made me the Laird of this castle and these lands. I will do as I see fit, whether you approve or not! You are no longer in charge of these decisions."

Willow looked up when she noticed the others had quietly

slipped in— Brody, Nahla, Sabina, and Skye. Molly brought Colin's plate over and set it before him. "Leave the wee shite alone, Stewart! Ye can't expect him to live his life to please ye and not himself! Mary would be terribly upset if she knew what ye were up to!"

She turned to MacDonnell. "And if ye gave two shites about yer own daughter, ye would not expect her to marry him. It's clear as the nose on yer face Colin is not the one she is in love with!"

MacDonnell looked to Sabina. "What the hell is this woman talking about?"

"I don't know, Father," she said and looked down as she wrung her hands worriedly.

The entire room erupted into the sounds of arguing.

Willow took a piece of bread from her plate, propped her elbow up, and chewed on it as the volume got even louder.

Suddenly, Colin roared over everyone else. "ENOUGH!" and the room fell silent.

MacDonnell's face became enraged. "My daughter will marry the Laird of this castle and these lands, or there will be war!"

Colin stood up and went to stand in front of him, equally enraged. "I refuse to be forcibly wed to a woman I was promised was a virgin while she carries another man's child!"

An audible gasp went up in the room.

"How dare ye accuse my daughter of such a thing!" fumed MacDonnell.

Finn smirked, threw his arm over the back of his chair, and looked over at Sabina who was now silently crying as Brody stared down at the floor, his eyes wide with fear. All the color had drained from his face. "Well lass, is it true? Are ye with child?"

All eyes turned to her. She wiped her face and swallowed hard as she looked at Brody.

"Answer him truthfully and end this nonsense once and for all!" ordered her father.

Sabina hesitated, closed her eyes, and slowly nodded.

The room erupted again.

Colin threw up his hands in frustration and shouted. "In my library! NOW!" he commanded and followed them out, leaving Willow, Skye, and Finn alone in the room.

"Well, this is an entertaining turn of events!" said Finn, thoroughly amused.

"Whose baby is she carrying?" whispered Skye.

"That would be Brody's!" replied Willow and pushed her plate away. "It seems they have fallen in love."

"Brody?" exclaimed Skye and laughed into her hand. "What do you think they will do now?"

Willow shrugged nervously. "I don't know. I just hope there is no bloodshed."

Colin appeared from the hall an excruciating half an hour later and blew out a long breath as she rushed into his arms. "Is it that bad?" she asked.

He frowned. "I am afraid there will be a wedding today after all. The MacLeod Laird will take his new bride, Sabina MacDonnell," he said solemnly.

"What?" she asked, dumbfounded, and tried to back away from him. "I thought—" He pulled her tighter and pressed his finger to her lips to quiet her. "I suppose I should go help my brother get ready for the ceremony."

"I—what?" she asked, confused.

Colin smiled. "I have relinquished my title as 'Laird' and passed it on to my little brother, Brody."

"You can do that?"

Colin shrugged. "I am the Laird, and I can do as I wish, or at least I was, and could, until just a few moments ago. I am fairly certain I won't miss the title or responsibilities."

Her eyes flew open wide. "Brody—is marrying— Sabina?"

"And the two of them could not be more pleased, although Brody is still reeling from the fact he is going to be a father," he smiled.

She threw her arms around him, and he lifted her off the ground. "Wait, what about Nahla? Won't her father want to marry her off to you?"

"We reached an agreement. She will have a MacLeod as a husband, but not until she is older. In the meantime, I worked out a little land deal in exchange for allowing her to stay here with her sister. That way, she can fall in love with one of our family members the way it is meant to be. After finding out Sabina was already with child, he was a little more willing to negotiate."

Willow's laughter turned into tears, and she embraced him.

"Speaking of weddings," he said and cleared his throat. "What do you say you let me make an honest woman out of you, so I won't have to lock you up in the bedchamber anymore?"

"Lock her up?" asked Skye with a horrific look on her face.

"You want to marry me?" asked an astonished Willow.

"Well, that's not how ye ask a woman to be your wife! For goodness sakes man, would it kill ye to be romantic for once?" fussed Finn who still sat at the table. "Get down on one knee and profess your love like a real man. Surely, she deserves that much!"

"Finn is right!" Skye grinned as she leaned against him. "You should listen to him. He knows how to treat a woman, and you could stand to learn a thing or two from him."

Colin laughed. "You two may have a point." He dropped to one knee and grasped her hand. "Willow Mason, you are the love of my life, and I feel like I have waited an eternity for you. Will you do me the honor of never leaving my side, or my bed, and be my wife?"

She nodded. "Yes, but I do have one condition."

He stood and looked troubled.

She took his face in her hands, "No one is watching us on our wedding night!"

He burst into laughter. "Agreed!" and he kissed her. He looked to Skye and Finn. "If you will excuse us, I think we need to celebrate." He swept her up in his arms and carried her out of the room. He stopped when Finn called out, "Willow? What was it ye wanted to say to the King?"

She looked over Colin's shoulder. "I think I would say, 'thank you for giving me such a wonderful gift'."

Finn nodded and grinned. "I think he would say, 'ye are very welcome' and he might just thank ye back," he winked and took Skye by the hand.

Brody and Sabina were married later in the day. The new Laird and his wife were incredibly happy with the new arrangement, while her father, however, remained unusually quiet during the affair. The two families gathered for the wedding feast after the ceremony, and Colin made sure the wine flowed freely in hopes some of the earlier tension would abate.

"Tell us about yourself," said Skye to Willow. "How did you and my brother end up meeting anyway?"

"Maybe that is a discussion best left for later," replied Willow behind her glass when she saw Aenghus MacDonnell glaring at her as he took a sudden interest in their conversation. "I would rather hear about you and Finn. I have a feeling it is quite the story."

Skye leaned over and Finn put his arm around her. "It was love at first sight," said Finn.

Skye kissed his cheek, her love for him unmistakable. "I decided to take a ride one day out to the Faerie Springs. It was rather warm, and the water was just too inviting, so I disrobed and decided to cool off. I took my time washing my hair in the waterfall, before diving in, and when I came back up, there was the most handsome man I had ever laid eyes on, sitting on the rocks, watching me. When I demanded he explain himself, he said he heard my singing and thought I must have been a beautiful siren luring him with my song because he could not help but be drawn to me. He then began to rattle off some story about the King of the Fae falling in love with a beautiful mortal woman he met in those very pools."

Finn took over. "Before I could even recite my narrative, she proceeded to throw a handful of pebbles at me and told me to shut my fecking mouth. She then called me a vile scoundrel and told me to turn around so she could dress. When I pointed out vile scoundrels had reputations to uphold, and I must politely decline because I would not want anyone to think I was an honorable man in any respect, she boldly walked out of the water onto the shore. She then decided to proudly stride right by me, as naked as the day she was born, and ask me if I liked what I saw. By the time she had dressed, I was hopelessly in love with her."

Skye laughed softly. "I got on my horse, and he rode exactly ten paces behind me until I reached the castle, reciting poetry and declaring his love for the 'siren of the Faerie Pool' the entire way. Once we came through the gates, he dismounted from his horse and informed me I would be his bride before the next full moon. When I told him, he was not only delusional, but full of shite, he pulled me into a kiss that made the rest of the world disappear, and even though I slapped him hard across the face, I knew in the moment all was lost and I would never want another."

Finn grinned. "She let me woo her for a full two weeks before I finally had enough, showed up in the main hall with a priest and a gown, and demanded she marry me that very moment."

Skye pinched his cheek. "Lucky for you, you had good taste in gowns, or I would have had to refuse you right there on the spot."

"That is the most romantic story I have ever heard in my life," said Willow with a smile.

"You don't think our story is romantic?" teased Colin.

"Well, you did mistake me for a whor—" she stopped herself when she looked in the direction of Aenghus MacDonnell and something caught her attention.

"Mistook ye for what?" asked Finn.

"Someone else," she mumbled. Her attention was on Sabina who had gotten up, excused herself, and ran toward the library looking very much as if she were about to be sick. She stood up and whispered to Colin. "I am going to check on Sabina. She looks a little ill. I will be right back."

When Willow found Sabina, she had just vomited and was sitting in one of the chairs in front of the fireplace with a bowl in her lap. "Morning sickness?" she asked sympathetically as she sat down across from her.

"Aye," replied Sabina. "Although I cannot imagine why they call it morning sickness when it lasts all day."

"Hopefully, it will pass soon."

Sabina looked over at Willow. "I want to thank ye for I feel like this is all yer doing. If not for ye, I would be very unhappily wed to Colin and not the one I genuinely love. I hope ye and I can become friends."

Willow took her hand. "I would like that very much."

Sabina smiled and stood, leaving the bowl by the door. "I should get back. We will talk soon."

Willow watched her go and waited until she was out of sight before speaking aloud, "I want you to know I can see you, and if you need help, I will do what I can."

A look of relief crossed the woman's face, and she raised her folded hands in front of her as if giving thanks to God.

"It is not I who needs help," said the specter as she wrung her hands and looked toward the main hall. "It is all of ye who are in danger."

12

CHAPTER TWELVE

"Who are you?" asked Willow.

"I am Abigail MacDonnell, wife of Aenghus MacDonnell. Sabina and Nahla are my daughters. Please! Ye must save my girls!"

"What are you talking about? They are in no danger from the MacLeods."

Abigail sat down in the chair Sabina just vacated. "Nay, they are not. It's their father who wishes to see them dead. Ye see, my husband is a despicable man, and he has despised our children since I bore them because they were girls."

Willow held up her hand, confused. "He has married off Sabina and agreed to leave Nahla here. That doesn't sound like a man who is trying to kill them."

"It is all a ruse. This wedding was just a means to an end. He wants this stronghold for his own nefarious purposes because of its location. He had planned to poison Sabina and Nahla at breakfast on the morning of their departure, use it as an excuse to slaughter every living MacLeod within these walls, and proclaim this castle his, knowing no one would challenge him on the basis his children had been murdered, but now his plans have slightly changed. Sabina already carrying a MacLeod heir in her belly played more to his advantage than he could have ever hoped for. He will spirit Sabina safely away to MacDonnell lands, murder Nahla, and make it appear the Laird ordered it to justify his attack."

"He was going to kill her, but Nahla beat him to it when she found Sabina and Brody together," whispered Willow to herself. Abigail looked at her questioningly, but Willow waved her off. "Wait! Why suddenly spare Sabina?"

"Because, if her child is the only surviving MacLeod heir left, by law, the child will inherit ALL the MacLeod lands and fortifications, not just this castle. In addition to that, not only will Aenghus claim proxy and rule these lands in the child's name, but he will make sure to raise him or her to do his bidding, that is if he lets the bairn live that long. Please, ye have to do something!" she pleaded.

Willow swallowed hard and looked in the direction of the celebration. "Would he be ruthless enough to do that to his daughters?"

Abigail closed her eyes. "He came here with the full intention of returning a childless man. He has chosen a bride of a mere sixteen years he intends to marry once he arrives back home, and he means for her to give him plenty of male heirs. God help her if she does not, for she will meet the same fate as I. It was the death of me."

A chilling realization washed over Willow. "How did you die?" she whispered, unsure if she wanted to know the answer.

"He took to the drink one night a few years ago and became enraged I had not given him another child since Nahla, and the bastard beat me to death. He made up a ridiculous story, telling everyone I was thrown from my horse and died from a broken neck, but there was not one soul who didn't know the truth. No one had the fortitude to challenge his word for fear of ending up the same way."

"I'm so sorry," said Willow.

Abigail looked at Willow with a look of desperation on her face. "Will ye save my girls?"

Willow nodded. "I will do all I can."

"Thank ye!" and she slowly dissipated.

Willow blew out a deep breath as her mind worked in overdrive. She had not stopped the fateful outcome of the MacLeod family, after all, just shifted some of the minor details. She needed to get Colin alone and tell him what she had learned, but she also had Aenghus MacDonnell watching her like a hawk.

Now that she knew how truly merciless and cold-hearted the bastard was, she would not make the mistake of underestimating him. As she stared into the flames of the fire, she heard Finn call out to her, "What are ye doing in here? The party is out there. I only came in here to acquire additional, stronger libations."

He went over to the desk and searched until he located a particular bottle of whiskey he was looking for. "Ah, success! Here it is!" He took notice of her pensive mood. "Are ye alright, lass?"

"No, I am not actually. Can you get Colin in here without raising any suspicion?"

Finn nodded. "Of course! I am the perfect man for the job!" He proceeded to the doorway, cleared his throat, and shouted out across the lively crowd, "Colin! Yer lass has requested yer presence! Something about wanting ye to tend to a certain ache needing immediate relief. She's spread out on the desk waiting for ye, and, by the looks of her, ye should hurry, or ye may find her trying to take care of it herself."

His words were met with a loud round of boisterous laughter and applause.

Willow's face burned red from embarrassment as she dropped her head into her hands. "I meant, discreetly and quietly!"

"Oh! Well, ye should have been more specific!" He winked impishly.

Willow laughed at him despite herself. "You are a hot mess,

you know that?"

"A hot mess? I will say I have been called much worse, my dear," he grinned as he poured a glass and handed it to her.

"Willow, what the devil?" demanded Colin as he came into the room.

"Close the door!" she said.

"May I please stay and watch?" asked Finn, excitedly.

"No, but you can stay and listen," she replied. "We might need your help."

"Ah, an even better prospect!"

Skye and Brody appeared just as Colin went to close the door. "It's my wedding day," said Brody, good-naturedly, "I am supposed to be the one sneaking off to 'relieve an ache'."

"You already snuck off," scolded Skye, trying to keep a straight face. "That's why your virtuous bride is with child!"

"Like you and Finn waited for your wedding night?" scoffed Brody and put his arm around his sister.

The playfulness faded when they saw the serious expression on Willow's face.

"What's going on?" questioned Colin as he went to her side.

"I just learned some alarming information. Aenghus MacDonnell plans on killing all of us."

"Well, that sounds like a terribly rude way to repay hospitality," snarked Finn and sipped from his glass.

"What do you mean? That can't be right," said Brody. "How did you come by this knowledge?"

Willow looked to Colin and spoke carefully, "The information came from a MacDonnell relative who is extremely near and dear to Aenghus and his daughters. I have my own special way of learning things, and I have no doubt it is the truth."

Colin gave her a peculiar look. His eyes widened when he realized what she meant.

Willow explained the previous plan and the new one as Colin sat on the arm of her chair, broodingly. "That is the day after tomorrow. We do not have much time to prepare."

"These men are firmly entrenched in our home," exclaimed Brody. "How can we possibly defend against this?"

Colin stroked his chin as he thought. "We will have to outsmart him instead. We protect Sabina and Nahla. If they are not at breakfast, they cannot be poisoned, and he won't have a reason to start a war."

"He would find another reason," assured Willow and downed her drink. "I get the distinct impression from my source he is hell-bent on this. I suppose it is too much to hope for the man to just drop dead of natural causes," she remarked sarcastically.

Finn refilled her glass. "Ye never know. Stranger things have happened."

When the doorknob rattled, Colin stood defensively. "We should table this until the morning when we are somewhere more private."

"Excellent idea," agreed Finn as he took Skye in his arms. "If our days are numbered, we should spend the night eating, drinking, being merry, and making love!"

Colin nodded. "Tomorrow then!"

"I thought I had stopped it," said Willow as she undressed down to her shift back in Colin's bedchamber. "I was certain of it!"

Colin unfastened his belt, removed his tartan, and tossed it on a nearby chair. "Who told you about this plot anyway?"

"Their mother. She also told me her dear husband beat her to death when she didn't give him a son."

"That bastard!" he mumbled under his breath as he pulled his shirt over his head and added it to the pile.

"What are we going to do?" she asked.

"We are forewarned and will be forearmed. With the information you learned, we will be ready." He took her in his arms and turned his full attention to removing the comb from her hair, letting her curls spill down, and running his fingers through them as he endearingly arranged them on her shoulders. "In the meantime, I think Finn had the right idea." He took her face in his hands and kissed her in earnest, before pushing the shift away from her shoulders, letting it fall to the floor.

13

CHAPTER THIRTEEN

The morning of the farewell breakfast, Colin watched Aenghus MacDonnell intently. The man appeared to be in good spirits— putting on quite the show as a father pleased with the union of the two families. Perhaps his mood had more to do with the fact he was looking forward to a bloody battle.

Around the room, MacDonnell's men were scattered about, mingling with MacLeods instead of keeping to themselves at one table as they would have normally done under any other circumstances. It seems they had strategically placed themselves in the most advantageous spots for a surprise attack.

Colin would never have taken notice of the concealed weapons he now saw if Willow had not warned them, and they would have been like lambs to the slaughter. He rested his hand on her trembling thigh beneath the table, giving it a comforting squeeze to reassure her things were well in hand, but the fear in her eyes was unmistakable. After informing Molly of the plot, she set about finding the planted MacDonnell in her kitchen and had discerned whom the woman was in under an hour.

After being confronted, the woman called Mandy, had broken down crying and confessed the entire scheme. MacDonnell held her seven-year-old son as a hostage and if she did not do his bidding, he would kill him. She was to obtain a pitcher with just enough wine for Nahla's glass, poison it with a vial she was given, serve it to her, and leave. Finn was able to ascertain the vial contained hemlock and enough poison to cause a dramatic, not to mention extremely painful, demise.

Once they uncovered the details, the siblings, along with Willow and Finn, spent the previous day coming up with a plan to create a different ending, purposefully leaving Stewart, Sabina, and Nahla in the dark.

Colin looked on as Mandy came in, poured Nahla's goblet, and left, nervously glancing over at Aenghus on the way out. As the old man watched her go, a sly smirk appeared on his face. Brody gave Colin a nod. He leaned over and kissed Willow on the cheek, then whispered in her ear, "Don't hesitate to use the blade I gave you to protect yourself and remember, no matter what happens, I love you!"

She grasped his hand tightly. "I love you, too. Be careful!"

Colin pushed his chair back and stood, before stumbling a bit and announcing loudly, "Family, friends! Please indulge me for a moment for there is something I would like to say." He picked up his goblet and moved around to stand in front of the long table where the family sat, as everyone gave him their full attention. "For far too long, the MacLeods and the MacDonnells have been on the verge of war, but the marriage between my brother and Sabina MacDonnell has now brought a welcome end to those hostilities." Colin stopped in front of Aenghus's place at the table and turned to face him; Stewart sat to his right and Nahla sat to his left. "I want to thank Laird MacDonnell for agreeing to this peace between our lands, even though things may have gotten off to a rocky start, but it has all ended well." Colin steadied himself with his hands on the table and shook it slightly.

"Ye are drunk!" said Stewart as he went to get up, but Skye caught his arm and silently directed him to remain seated with her eyes. He slowly leaned back with a puzzled look on his face.

"I would ask all of you to join me in raising a glass to him and his commitment to what he has brought forth here this day. May his deeds be returned tenfold." As Colin raised his glass, he staggered again, intentionally knocking Aenghus's glass over to spill onto Nahla's gown.

She jumped to her feet and began to shake off her dress as Aenghus cursed aloud, "Damn it, MacLeod, ye clumsy oaf!" MacDonnell's men instantly tensed, especially his right-hand man, Seth MacCain, and the room went silent when they heard him raise his voice. Colin called for a servant to clean it up and turned to Nahla. "Milady, my sincerest apologies for being a graceless beast. I am afraid whiskey was not the best drink of choice so early this morning." He tried to bow sincerely but wobbled.

"Why don't I help ye find something else to wear?" offered Molly who happened to be close by with a towel. "Come on, dear, we will fix ye right up and have ye back down here in no time to bid a proper farewell to yer father."

"Why don't you go with her?" said Brody to Sabina and helped her up.

"NAY!" shouted Aenghus. "They will remain until the morning meal is finished!"

The three women hesitated, but Brody waved them on. "They will only be a few moments. I am sure Nahla wants to look her best for her goodbye to you, and in the meantime, we will have more time to drink! All of you, except my brother, that is, who has obviously had enough!" he laughed and waved his glass in the direction of the men at the table. "You men don't mind more wine, do you?" he asked good-naturedly, and the somewhat tense crowd relaxed.

Colin turned back to Aenghus. "Let's not cry over spilled wine, shall we?" and he picked up Nahla's glass. "Here, please accept this one with my apologies." He held it up to Aenghus, who looked over to where it came from and eyed the glass warily. "Well, go on! We don't want to waste a perfectly good drink, and

I know you will not insult me by not raising a glass to my words." Colin suddenly straightened his back and stood unmoving, plainly sober as he waited for MacDonnell to make his choice.

Aenghus narrowed his eyes at Colin when he realized Colin knew exactly what was going on and he, in fact, was the one being played.

"Go on, Aenghus," called one of the MacDonnell men who had found one of the lovely MacLeod ladies, a cousin, most interesting and was giving her his full attention. "Ye might as well drink up their wine so it will leave us more of our own for the journey home.

"Yes!" said Colin. "Drink it all down in a toast to your good health!"

Aenghus snatched the glass from him, looked down into it, and stood. He raised the glass to his lips, looked Colin square in the eye, and proceeded to throw it onto his shirt. "My sincerest apologies," he said mockingly. "It seems I am as clumsy an oaf as ye are! Forgive me!"

Colin's jaw tightened and he frowned at Aenghus with a vexed expression on his face for a long moment before bursting into laughter. He turned in the direction of the rest of the tables as he wrung his shirt out and roared even louder. "Well, it seems we are now all one big happy family of clumsy oafs! Let's hope the next generation is born a bit more graceful for the sake of the wine bill."

The room erupted into applause at his words, and Colin moved over to where Willow sat. "Please!" declared Colin loudly as he smiled at her, for all to hear as he picked up his glass as well as Willow's. "Take my wine glass as an offering of goodwill." He handed it to Aenghus who reluctantly accepted it from him. "To new beginnings!" Colin drank down his wine. "To new beginnings!" snarked Aenghus and angrily took his seat.

"To new beginnings!" said Finn to the crowd with his raised glass. "Drink! Eat! Enjoy!"

Aenghus's face darkened when he realized his plan did not work, and he sat, seething, as Colin returned to his seat next to Willow.

"How long?" she whispered as she took his hand under the table.

"Finn said it would not be long at all," he replied as he blew out a deep breath. "And according to Skye, he is the best with tonics she has ever seen. Listen to me, if things go badly, immediately run to our room, and bolt the door. Do not open it for anyone you do not know."

"I want to stay with you!"

"I know, my love, but I need you safe. If there is a battle here today, I cannot protect myself or my family if I am distracted because I am worried about you. Please! Promise me!"

She closed her eyes and gave him a nod. They both looked up when Sabina and Nahla returned and took their seats. After nearly fifteen minutes had passed, Colin looked at Finn with widened eyes and a quizzical expression on his face.

Offering a sly smirk, Finn merely raised his glass to him and winked.

Deciding he wanted the castle once and for all and no longer caring if he had a legitimate reason to attack, Aenghus stood up and cleared his throat. The room went silent as his men looked to him for instruction.

Brody leaned over and whispered to Sabina, who suddenly went ghostly pale and swallowed hard.

Colin turned and kissed Willow before tightening his grip on the hilt of his sword concealed beneath the table, ready to move in an instant.

Finn was surprisingly calm, his elbow propped on the table with his chin resting in one palm, a self-assured grin on his face as he lovingly pressed his lips to Skye's hand.

Aenghus sneered as he looked around. The room fell silent as his men waited for the signal to attack. As he opened his mouth to speak, a peculiar thing happened. His hands suddenly flew to his chest, clawing at his heart as if in pain. His face turned a scarlet red, his body convulsed twice, and he fell face forward into his breakfast plate.

In the blink of an eye, Aenghus MacDonnell was dead.

Everyone remained frozen in disbelief, unsure of what would

come next.

Stewart finally was the first to move and shouted for the healer. "Help me!" he commanded, spurring Brody and Colin to action. They each took an arm and laid the deceased on his back on the floor.

Sabina pulled Nahla away from the scene, wrapping her arms around her and shielding her eyes. Skye and Willow moved over to join them, inching closer to a door that could be used as an escape route if necessary.

Colin, Brody, and Finn strategically positioned themselves between the women and the others. Some of the MacDonnell men rushed to their leader's side just as Samuel appeared. The healer loosened his shirt and checked his breathing as Stewart explained to him what happened.

"He just…fell over, right into his plate!"

"There is nothing I can do for him. He is already gone," Samuel pronounced. "Did he by chance have issues with his heart?"

Abigail MacDonnell's anxious spirit appeared behind Willow. "Get Sabina to tell him Aenghus's father and brother both died of heart issues and, for the love of God, tell her to look a wee bit more like an aggrieved lass who has just lost her father!".

"Right!" Willow nodded. She sidled up to Sabina, grasped her hand and whispered in her ear. Sabina's eyes widened when she realized her error. Stepping forward, she cleared her throat and addressed Samual, "His father, my grand sire and his brother, my beloved uncle, both died of heart issues and at verra early ages, as I recall," she announced before letting out a little cry and rushing to his side, kneeling to take his head in her hands. "Oh, Father! Why did ye have to leave us?" she said, covering her face as she feigned a wail that reverberated throughout the grand hall. "What will become of us?"

Colin nudged Brody with his shoulder causing him to lose his balance. He looked at his brother annoyed. "What the…?" Colin cut his eyes to Sabina and tilted his head. Brody suddenly took his meaning. Joining his wife, he placed his hands on her shoulders, comfortingly. "There, there! Everything will be alright!"

"Samuel?" asked Colin. "What say you?"

The old man shook his head and stood. "It would appear his heart just gave out. It was simply time to meet his maker. At least the poor soul didna suffer. We should all be so fortunate when our time comes, I suppose."

MacDonnell's men looked to Seth MacCain, unsure of what to do. He seemed at a loss as well.

Brody helped Sabina to her feet. "My wife is upset over the loss of her father. I need to take her upstairs. You are welcome to move him to our chapel until arrangements can be made." The pair started toward the door.

"Milady!" Seth called out to Sabina as he looked down at Aenghus, "Yer father had no male heirs. Ye are the eldest daughter. By our own MacDonnell tradition, ye are now the head of the MacDonnell clan. What would ye like us to do?"

Sabina stared back at him in disbelief. "Me?" She looked to Brody and then around the room at the men, clearly anxious to cut down the MacLeods on her word. She gently touched Brody's face and nodded. "Because the land and yer loyalties now belong to me, they also now belong to my husband's family, the MacLeods. Ye will do whatever my husband asks of ye; he speaks for both of us as we are now, and always, one united family."

"Aye, milady!" responded Seth through gritted teeth. "Whatever ye say!"

Brody slipped his arm around her waist and led her out, stopping to take Nahla's hand as they went.

Colin took Willow in his arms and breathed a sigh of relief, watching as the MacDonnell's men started to move his body out.

"What just happened?" she asked.

"Finn mixed something to make it look like his heart simply gave out so there would be no question of poison," he stated quietly.

"And MY husband is the best at that sort of thing," Skye whispered.

"Remind me not to piss him off," Willow replied.

Finn came up behind Skye and put his arms around her waist. "And the cream on the top is the MacDonnell lands are now

MacLeod lands. How is that for an ironic twist of fate?"

"How does that work again?" asked Willow.

"It falls to Sabina and only secondly to Nahla; she is now married to a MacLeod and carrying the heir for both families. Their son will rule it all."

As the room started to clear, Willow saw something out of the corner of her eye. As she looked closer, she saw a sight she had never seen before. Aenghus MacDonnell's spirit standing over his body, ranting and raving at the fates. His eyes narrowed in on her. As he started toward her, a black wisp of smoke suddenly appeared next to him. The little puff quickly twisted and morphed before forming into a hand, then two, then ten, all reaching for him, grasping at his ankles before moving up his body to his arms. Ten exploded into a hundred and began to overtake him.

He tried to fight them off, but they continued to multiply until there were so many, the outline of his spirit was the only feature to be seen. The hands began to shift downward, dragging him to the floor, and then through the stones until he disappeared, screaming and writhing in agony as he went.

Willow covered her mouth with her hand, aghast at the scene she watched unfold.

Abigail appeared over her shoulder and whispered in her ear. "Those were the souls of the men he killed unjustly over the years. They will now have their revenge." She smiled. "Thank ye, Willow, for saving my girls. I will always be grateful to ye, and now I can move on to a better place. Be well." Abigail MacDonnell took a step back and Willow watched as her form dissipated into a warm golden light. Peacefulness filled the void where she had stood once she moved into the next world.

Willow's eyes drifted upwards. "Godspeed, Abigail...and thank you!"

The following day, Sabina ordered her father's body to be taken back to the MacDonnell lands to be buried. They all traveled together as a family and returned a few days after the funeral.

Willow decided to go for a walk while Colin and Brody were locked up in the library with Sabina brokering a plan for her inheritance to keep the peace. She was smelling one of the roses growing near Mary's grave when she noticed Nahla alone on the top walk of one of the outer walls overlooking the loch. The poor girl had been through a great deal the past week, and Willow felt a sudden urge to check on her. Sabina had decided it was best to leave out the details of their father's treachery for the sake of sparing her sister the heartache, so she had no idea of what fate he had planned for her. When Willow found her, Nahla was leaned forward with her head down as if in deep thought.

"Are you alright?" she asked gently as she approached.

Nahla's head snapped up, but she remained with her back

turned.

"I know it has been a tough time, and I just wanted to see how you were dealing with things."

"This is all yer fault," said Nahla vehemently. "Everything would have been fine if ye had never come here."

Willow was taken aback as Nahla turned to face her. She was alarmed to see the young girl clenching a dagger in her hand, one she had just pulled from the belt around her gown. "Sabina would be married to Colin, and I would be married to Brody, but instead, ye are to be married to Colin and my sister is wed to the man I love."

"You love Brody?" asked Willow, confused.

Nahla took a step towards her. "He would have been mine. I met him when he came to arrange Sabina's marriage, and I knew we were meant for each other as soon as we were introduced. He was so sweet to me, especially when we danced at his arrival supper. He told me I was a beautiful girl and the man who would be my husband would be the luckiest alive. I was so full of joy when Father told me he intended to see us wed."

"He is in love with your sister and has been since they met," retorted Willow, casting an uneasy glance toward her hand gripping the knife.

Nahla moved closer, and Willow backed away from her toward the outer stone wall.

"He doesn't love her. She threw herself at him, only seduced him to spite his brother, and Brody only married her because Colin found out she carried his child. If Colin hadn't learned about the bairn, Sabina would have married him and raised the babe as his own. By now, I would have been wed to Brody. Everyone would have been happy, but ye ruined it all!"

"Sabina didn't want Colin, and they would have never been happy together." Willow felt the wall at her back. She looked over to see the three-story drop into the loch with trepidation.

"They would have learned to love each other for the sake of the child!" she shouted bitterly. "I was the one who convinced Sabina to not reveal the truth and to let him believe they conceived on their wedding night. It would have worked if ye had not been such a whore and led him astray! Brody and I would be together now as Father planned. He told me before we arrived here, he intended for me to not return home with him, and I would be joining the MacLeods shortly—he would see me placed at Brody's side."

Willow realized Nahla was not in her right mind. Perhaps, she was naive or maybe she was more like her father than anyone had known. "That is not what he meant! Your father intended to poison you and use it as an excuse to murder everyone here. You would have been at Brody's side in an early grave had he had his way!"

"LIES!" screeched Nahla and she lunged at Willow with the knife.

Willow caught her arm and managed to sidestep as the girl attempted to plunge the blade into her chest.

Savagely, Nahla let out a shrill and swung again, this time forcing Willow to the open edge of the walk, which was a straight drop to the ground inside the fortress wall. Willow fell to her knees and scrambled to get away from the ledge, knocking a few loose stones below and catching the attention of some of the men in the courtyard.

"Nahla, you have to listen to me!" Willow scuttled to the safety of the parapet. "You are confused. You don't understand!"

"I understand if ye are gone, I can put things right. I understand all I will have to do is get rid of Sabina, and then I can take her place as Brody's wife."

"You would murder your sister and her unborn child for unrequited love?"

"Brody loves me!"

"No! He does not!" shouted Willow, inching toward the wooden steps going down. "He loves Sabina, and you will make a poor substitute!"

"More of yer lies!" cried a crazed Nahla as she rushed to her and raised the blade above her head. "I will hear no more from ye!"

"She's right!" called Brody from the top of the stairs where he and Colin had appeared. "I love Sabina!"

Nahla stopped and turned to stare at him as he worked his way toward her. "I am sorry if you somehow got the wrong idea, but it is your sister, and her only, I love."

Nahla shook her head in disbelief. "But ye told me I was beautiful, and my husband would be a lucky man."

"And he will be, whoever he is!" Brody and Colin shuffled their way toward Nahla.

Willow crawled backward until she was in the safety of her lover's arms.

"Are you hurt?" whispered Colin as he pulled her away and embraced her tightly as if holding on for dear life.

"I am fine, but she is not!"

Brody held out his hand when he saw Colin had Willow out of harm's way. "You will find a man who you love and who will return that love, but it is not me. Please, give me the dirk, and let's go inside to talk about this."

She looked down at his hand, disoriented and unhinged. "Ye never loved me?"

"I am sorry, but no."

Nahla nodded her head and tossed the knife away. As they all breathed a collective sigh of relief, Nahla turned to her left, calmly walked to the outer wall—and threw herself over the side.

"NAHLA!" screamed Willow and ran to where she had stood.

Colin and Brody leaned over the side to look for her but could only see the water below. Colin shouted for the men to search the loch as he took Willow by the arms.

"She was not in her right mind!" cried Willow as she buried her face against his chest.

"I know!" he whispered and kissed the top of her head.

That evening, at sunset, Willow stood on the bank of the loch, searching the top of the water for any sign of the young girl.

"Our men have found no trace of her," said Colin as he came up behind her. "Have you seen her spirit?"

Willow shook her head. "No, I have not. How is Sabina?"

"She is upset, but when we told her what happened, she understood. Her mother made her promise to look after Nahla, not just because she was her little sister, but because Nahla sometimes had issues distinguishing reality in some matters. She was not surprised in the least, and to be quite honest, for a moment, I think I saw a slight tinge of relief on her face when we told her."

"It's just such a shame!" She stepped to him, and he wrapped his arms around her before guiding her toward the castle.

"I am only glad you are safe. I think I am going to have to marry you just to keep you in my bed at all times. You get into too much trouble when you leave it."

"Your bed does sound like a tempting place to be!" She grinned.

"As a matter of fact, I think you should be there right now," he laughed and swept her up in his arms, kissing her as if for the first time.

14

CHAPTER FOURTEEN

Willow and Colin married three weeks later in an intimate ceremony in the rose garden. Willow smiled when she caught sight of Mary standing next to Stewart during the wedding, as they had their first kiss as husband and wife.

After the ceremony, they gathered in the main hall for a huge celebration. While Colin was off having a word and a drink with Brody, Finn held out his hand to Willow. "Allow me to offer my sincerest 'congratulations'," he smiled and handed her a glass. "They two of ye seem very happy."

"We are!"

Finn escorted her to a chair and sat down in the one next to her. "I was hoping ye might tell me the story ye mentioned when we first met."

"Now?" She laughed.

Finn flipped his hand in the air. "Oh, just hit the highlights. I do love a good tale, and it seems yer groom and my bride are off and about, so why not?"

Willow sipped her glass and suddenly felt very strange.

Finn leaned close to her ear and said, "Tell me a story of what is to come, and what the King of Fae and Fate has done."

Willow shook her head.

"It's alright, my dear. It is just a little potion to get you to tell me everything and then forget this conversation. There is nothing in it to harm ye."

The entire story spilled out and when she was done, he downed his drink and smiled.

"Yer groom is looking for ye," he said.

"Oh, yes! What were we talking about again?" Willow asked as if coming out of a trance.

"Just how happy ye two are."

"That was it!" she said. "If you will excuse me!"

"Of course, my dear."

Finn watched her go to her new husband, and his own love, speaking to her father. Stewart was ill and he would not live out the year. He encouraged her to spend as much time with her father as she could before his time was done. He loved Skye more than anything in this world, and he was pleased he would never have to wipe her tears for grieving the loss of her entire family from one senseless battle.

His spell must have worked better than expected, according to the recount Willow had just given him. He had no memory of it himself because the carnage had been prevented and there would be no need to cast it now. That happened on occasion when destinies and fates were changed, and it could not be avoided. Corrections would sometimes have to be made, and this situation must have been one of them.

At any rate, the MacLeod line would now carry on for generations to come, getting an earlier start than any of them realized. Willow already carried Colin's son, even though she didn't know it yet. He had just sensed it, the bairn having been conceived the night before, and they were going to have their hands full with that one.

Skye waved at him; he blew her a kiss. She too was with child and didn't know it yet. He knew she would want to surprise him, and he would not deprive her of the pleasure. Their daughter would be a red-headed, green-eyed girl with a sharp tongue, just like her mother. The MacLeod women were a force to be reckoned with, and he was looking forward to this one's arrival into the world, especially since she would be the first child he ever conceived with a mortal...and she would have HIS Fae blood in her veins.

Yes, he had full-Fae children with Oona, but he had never allowed his seed to impregnate a human before now. He had never loved anyone as he did Skye, even giving himself completely to her and taking the time to live a life as a man among them. Their little girl would liven things up a bit and make life a little more interesting, especially coupled with Willow and Colin's son who would have the same gift as his mother.

Aye, the MacLeod family would be growing by leaps and bounds and were in no danger of fading into history. He smiled, looked down at his empty glass, and refilled it with an inconspicuous wave of his hand. Being the King of the Fae did have some advantages after all.

EPILOGUE

Nahla's eyes fluttered open, and she found herself staring at the ceiling of a house. Pushing up on her arms, she realized she was in a warm, comfortable bed dressed in only her shift. The last thing she remembered was going over the side of the castle wall after Brody told her he did not love her. She had intended to die, but it seemed fate had other plans for her. Throwing her legs over the side, she heard voices in the other room. "Who is there?" she called.

Seth MacCain appeared in the doorway. "Milady! It is good to see ye awake."

"What happened and why am I alive?"

Seth moved to a small table, poured her a glass of wine, and handed it to her. "I had returned to the MacLeod lands to try and reason with your sister about these maddening plans of hers to turn over the MacDonnell lands to the MacLeods, but she refused to hear me out. I saw ye go over the side, and I fished ye out of the loch before anyone could see. I brought ye here to one of the houses on yer father's hunting grounds. Ye see, the rest of the men and I think yer sister a traitor for giving everything over to our enemies so easily when yer father planned to take everything from them. As we see it, she has forsaken her clan and, since there is another heir with as much right as she, we want ye to lead us."

"Ye should have let me die," she said as she looked away.

"Ye are the daughter of the great warrior, Aenghus MacDonnell!" Seth fell to his knee. "Avenge yer father, take yer rightful place and yer revenge upon those who have wronged ye. Lead us against the MacLeods, help us take back yer lands, and we will serve ye as no other. I, personally, will serve all yer needs, whatever they may be, and however ye wish. It will be an honor to attend such a beautiful woman." He took her hand and kissed it.

Nahla looked down at the handsome man, surprised by his words and his affection. He lifted his head, and she touched his face lovingly as if seeing him for the first time—and she smiled.

The End...

or is it?

ABOUT THE AUTHOR

Tempie W. Wade, a Virginia native, is the award-winning author best known for her Timely Revolution Book Series, a captivating time-travel adventure that blends significant historical events from the Revolutionary War with ancient Celtic Fae lore.

Embarking on her writing journey in 2018 at the age of forty-seven, she lends credence to the old adage that "it's never too late to start something new." Since then, she has published ten novels, spanning various genres, including historical fiction, historical fantasy, and gothic fantasy. Her debut novel, A Timely Revolution, earned the distinction of Best Historical Fantasy at the 2019 American Book Fest American Fiction Awards.

The Timely Revolution Book Series is a work of historical fiction/fantasy based during the Revolutionary War with the added element of Celtic Fae lore.

The first book, A Timely Revolution, won Best Historical Fantasy in the American Book Fest American Fiction Awards for 2019. Books are available on Amazon.

The Timely Revolution Book Series in Order:

Book One-A Timely Revolution

Book Two-More

Book Three-The Complicated Life of Maggie MacGregor

Book Four-Timely Revelations

Book Five-The Steep Cost of Fate

Book Six-Secrets and Lies

Book Seven-Children of the Gods

Book Eight-TBA

Stand-Alone Books:

A Spy Among Them

Where Witches Lie

The Purveyor

For more information, please visit
www.TempieWade.com

www.ingramcontent.com/pod-product-compliance
Lightning Source LLC
Chambersburg PA
CBHW020758250626
47155CB00003B/1141